A SHADE OF SINFUL

MAY SAGE AS ALEXI BLAKE

A SHADE OF SINFUL

A Seven Kingdom Standalone Novel

By Alexi Blake

Cover by Clarissa Yeo
Photography by Michelle Lancaster
Edited by Theresa Schultz
Proofread by Virginia Tesi Carey
May Sage © 2022

The Kingdoms
of
Xhera

*The Seven
Kingdomgs*

1. Ravelyn
2. Flaur
3. Dorath
4. Anderkan
5. Vanimir
6. Darklands
7. The Eternal
   Realms

Five

To all of the young, thirsty minds who still feel salty that Dramione isn't canon.

I got you.

ONE GHOST AFTER THE NEXT

C ommitting a murder at a funeral might be uncouth—doubly so, given the fact that the woman I'd love to stab is the corpse's own daughter.

"I can't believe she's here," Alva mutters between her teeth, affronted on my behalf.

I remain silent, eyes forward, ignoring the familiar red flash of hot anger rising to the surface.

Neleda Stovrj-Rhodes is as beautiful as ever, clad in refined garments suitable for her new title. The duchess is the picture of elegance and sophistication. She sticks out like a sore thumb in the muck. To look at her blonde mane, falling in gentle waves out of her feathered headdress, and her black velvet cloak sparkling with diamonds, I'd never guess she was born right here in the undercity. I'd never guess she gave birth to a child and promptly forgot she ever existed.

I'm not being fair. She's visited three times in

nineteen years, bringing presents I soon pawned and promises she never kept.

I don't purposely keep an ear out for anything about her, but the undercity's rumor mill runs fast and my crew likes to babble. I heard about Neleda's marriage on the day the banns were read six months ago. It was only a week later that the guards started to storm my territory, looking for Helyn Stovrj, the duchess's "lost" little girl. Like I'd been misplaced, not left to rot. I wonder what lies she spun for her new husband. Did she tell him I ran away?

I don't care much. I might have occasionally thought I needed her as a child, but I survived just fine without her. Grandma Lyn did her best, and when her best wasn't enough, I stole, I cheated, and I lied to feed both of us. Now, I lead one of the best crew of misfits in the undercity, despite my young age. I'm doing just fine. There's nothing she could offer that might tempt me to let her into my life.

I don't even blame her, not truly. Everyone wishes they could crawl out of the poverty-ridden undercity, too hot in the summer, freezing cold during the long winter nights, and stinky year-round. Legitimate jobs are scarce, and none pay even half the bills. Women pop out dozens of kids just to have some help around the house. None can stay in school much past age twelve, because they need to get jobs and contribute to the household. No one truly gets out. Neleda is one in a million, the tale every little girl tells herself at night. The undercity rat who became a duchess of Ravelyn. I can admire her for it. I can even admit that in her shoes, I might have made the same choice, no matter how much I despise her.

She had the gall to come to the funeral. I should have expected it. For months, she's looked for me in vain. I am a shadow in these sinuous streets, only seen when I wish to be, and never caught. She knew I'd be here today though, to say goodbye to the only mother I ever knew.

The master of ceremonies invites me to speak, and applause thunders across the neighborhood square as I jump down from the roof of the Pillar church, carefully calculating every step: the gutter first, then a window, and I perch atop a gargoyle before the last leap. I land in a low crouch and the crowd yells in delight.

I enjoy my mother's horrified gasp, on the front line. *Yes, Neleda. You birthed a true street urchin.*

I'm not one for heedless displays, much preferring to operate in the dark and the quiet, but if I have to be seen, I'll do it right.

Alva and Khel follow my descent and a few steps stand behind me, keeping their hoods low on their eyes. I remove mine, my tangled hair braided out of my face. I'm told I owe the copper hue to Grandma Lyn, though she had thin silver-white hair for as long as I've known her, which is all my life.

The assembly screams the only name I answer to these days.

"Hel! Hel! Hel!"

I lift a hand and they fall silent.

I get it. As a child, I worshipped the crews, too. I would have been right here, screaming, if one of their leaders appeared in broad daylight. But today isn't about me, or about the Glitter Lane. It's about the only woman who ever loved me.

"Grandma Lyn," I call, my voice traveling across the square, "had a long life and died in her bed after too much ale at the pub, as befits a true Stovrj." Those who knew her best laugh, and the others cheer. "Today is a celebration of seventy-eight winters well lived. In this fatal game called life, Lyn won without screwing anyone else in the process." More applause and nods of agreement. "She wedded one husband, buried him after a foolish street war, and reared two girls still alive." My eyes settle on my mother for only one moment. "How many can boast such achievements?"

"Hail Lyn!"

"Lyn Stovrj, queen of the lane!"

It kills me that I have to share this moment, a moment that belongs to the undercity, to the streets Lyn so loved, with her treacherous daughter, but I'm not about to cut her farewell short because of Neleda. So I do what I must. I start to sing, at first into the silence, then to the sound of slow, rhythmic claps, and finally, with the entire square screaming along with me.

We give Lyn the goodbye she deserves.

I watch my mother shed a single tear and I want to slap it off her smooth skin. She doesn't deserve to grieve for a woman she didn't know. Lyn Stovrj is mine, not hers.

I daydream of spitting in her face, of punching her repeatedly.

That's the redhead in me—at least, so Grandma Lyn used to say. It serves me well, for the most part.

I would have retreated to the roofs at the end of the song, if it wouldn't have made me look a coward. Damn my pride, but I have to stand my ground as the duchess approaches me.

"I thought you might be dead," she sniffles, "when no news came from my search."

I chuckle, highly amused. "What I am is worthy of loyalty, Mother. Don't come into my domain and ask my people to betray me to the likes of you."

My second and third close in, standing right behind me, as though they believe I might need help against the small, delicate flower. And they're right. They'll have to hold me back if she says one word out of tune, lest I become hunted for the murder of a noble.

"I don't want—" she starts.

So funny. "Your wants are of no relevance to me, Duchess."

She huffs and winces. "By the gods, the words fail me. I'm not here to fight you. I have a proposal, Helyn. There is a place for you at my side. My husband cannot have children. You'd be his heir. You'd have everything you've ever dreamed of. You don't even need to see me."

This offer surprises me, and usually nothing does.

"Mother said you wished you could learn magik as a child. Is it still true?" Neleda takes one step closer than what I should allow. "You can study it at Five. I'm sure you can catch up to everyone else. You were always so smart, Helyn."

"Hel," I say, rejecting the name she gave me.

Five. She's offering a place at the university teaching kings and queens to *me*. Me, the street rat, the thief, and the shadow. And beyond that, she's dangling a duchy. In a remote, frozen kingdom, but a duchy all the same.

Five years ago, I would have killed for this dream.

Now, I just want her gone. "Go home, Mother. Take another man to your bed to give that duke an heir. Who knows? He might even enjoy watching."

CHAPTER TWO
DANGEROUS SCHEMES

T inherited the underground hideout from the
previous leader of the Claws Crew when she
retired two years ago. I've barely made any
changes, though the red drapes and dark tapestries are
hardly to my taste. Truth be told, I don't care much
what the den looks like. It's just a place to sleep, and
after days of work in the city, I'm not fussy so long as I
get a vaguely flat surface.

Khel offers to take the first watch in front of the
door leading to the tunnels. No one has ever found the
den, but if they did, we'd see a sign of light or hear noise
from the tunnel. We can escape out back.

It's Alva's turn to cook. Instead of humming and
babbling merrily about a job well done, as she normally
would, she stands in front of the stove in silence.

We did have a great day. After the funeral this
morning, we tailed a shipment driving through the
canals, up toward Whiteviews, a rich neighborhood
uptown. The vessel was well guarded, by both ground

and water patrols, but we got aboard it when the boat passed under the alley-bridge.

My policy is to never take enough to be noticed. It wouldn't do to swipe all of their shipments and drive the wealthy owners to send the guards up to us. Today, it was grain—rice, wheat, barley. Nothing fancy, but it keeps if well preserved, and we'll need it come winter.

Alva ran part of it to the orphanage where she grew up, and Khel distributed some to members of the crew —our errand boys, runners, scouts, and traders. The rest, we dropped off at the flea market on Glitter Lane. There's a community table we can load. Anyone in need can help themselves.

We've had better days, but we've certainly had worse. At least no one got shot at or magiked into a toad.

"Out with it, then." I know my second well enough to recognize when she's pissed at me. "Better you spit at me than in the goulash."

Alva doesn't hesitate to give me a piece of her mind. "How can you be this selfish?"

I'm too astounded to think of a reply. I'm no stranger to selfishness, same as anyone, but I can't say any of my actions were about putting myself first today.

"You're given something on a silver platter the rest of us kill for," she continues. "A position of power! A chance at a life of consequence!" Her voice rises. "Dammit, Helyn, you could make a real difference, give the undercity a voice among the rulers of this realm, and you dare refuse?"

I'm taken aback and hurt by each word. Probably because they ring true to my ears. Alva doesn't get the whole picture. She might know about my history, but she doesn't understand Neleda the way I do. "You don't know what you're talking about."

"I know today all we achieved was giving a bag of rice and dried beans per family in one out of the fifteen quarters in the undercity. We've fed them for a week, and we could have gotten killed for our efforts. The nobles up there? They can vote to give us enough water in the summer, and affordable heat in the winter. They can decide to build an orphanage and just like that—" She snaps her fingers in my face. "A hundred orphans cared for. Fed, clothed, taken off the street, educated. Dammit, Hel."

I'm not listening so much as straining to remain calm. When I think I can talk without reaching for my dagger or punching my closest friend, I say, "When I was seven, my mother came and cried about missing me so much she was going to stay put and never let me go. It lasted one week. Then she begged Grandma Lyn for money and was gone the next day. When I was eleven, she said she got a nice, sweet gig in a pub uptown, and she could get me a job with her. That pub? It was a brothel."

Alva gasps. She didn't know that. We met much later, after I'd started making a name for myself in the streets, and the crew looked my way. I've not volunteered the information before, though I made no secret of my contempt for the woman who gave birth to me.

Khel doesn't seem surprised, either because he has ears in every lane, or because he knows my mother better than I.

Both of my companions are older than me, but Alva's only twenty-five. Khel has ten years on her, which makes him only a couple of years younger than Neleda. He knows her from her days in the undercity, at least by reputation.

"Shit, Hel. I'm sorry."

"That I'm related to the bitch?" I scoff. "Me too. Nothing happened to me. Lyn arrived while she was packing my shit, screamed Neleda out of the house, and told her never to come back. But she did. She came back when I was fifteen, wounded by a lover who'd found her with another man. She stayed a month that time because she needed to heal up. A month, during which she swore up and down that she'd do better, be better, that we'd finally be a family." By then, I didn't believe a word out of her treacherous mouth. I'd just stayed out of her way.

The Claws Crew had let me in, so I was out most of the time anyway, trying to scavenge or steal whatever I could get my hands on. "Then, she was gone again. Neleda *lies*. That's what she does. I can't trust a word she says, and I sure as fuck can't entrust my future to her. The only thing she cares about is what she can *get* out of me."

Grandma Lyn would be proud that I managed to keep my voice even at all points, though I'm still seething. Sure, I understand her point of view, but after everything we've gone through together, Alva should trust my judgement. If I thought for one second that I could make an actual difference to our people, I'd be out of here in the blink of an eye. She must know that.

My second lowers her amber eyes to her feet. "Sorry, boss. It sounded..." She bites her lip. "It sounded good —her offer."

"Too good to be true," I agree.

She nods and returns her attention to the fragrant food.

We take turns cooking, and everyone looks forward to Alva's days. Her dad ran one of the boarding houses down by the harbor, before his death, and his cook showed her a thing or two in her youth.

Khel speaks from the entrance, gaze fixed on the tunnel. "Maybe..." He hesitates. "You owe it to yourself to find out."

Khel's not one to waste words, often content to go days on end without using his voice, and I don't think I've ever heard him say anything quite this cryptic. "Find out what?"

"If your mother is lying this time." He only glances at me for one second before facing the tunnel again.

"Neleda is a street rat, whatever feathers she dons these days. She'll con and lie to survive, same as the rest of us. Now, she's made it to the top. Married into money. She *could* be trying to pull you out. You're her daughter, Hel."

All my instincts tell me to dismiss his opinion. Trusting Neleda Stovrj would be foolish.

"Khel has a point." Alva's quick to take his side, though they usually can't agree that water's wet. "I say we approach this as we would any job. If this was anyone else, we'd stake out the mark, check if their story adds up. Then, if everything is legitimate, we'd take the assignment."

Except there's no we. This isn't something I could do with my crew. If I end up accepting Neleda's offer, I'll be on my own, in her territory.

I don't like this. Not even a little bit. "She doesn't live here," I remind them. "In the undercity, we're home. We can move unseen; surveillance isn't a problem. If she's uptown in a fancy house, it's way too far out of our comfort zone. There'd be guards, too. And she could already be back in the north, to Ravelyn, if she rushed home in a hovercraft."

"She tried to stake you out for six months," Khel reminds me. "She's still in Magnapolis."

I glance between my two friends, one hopeful, the other, as careful as ever.

They're right. We should try to work out what she really wants out of me. I'm not sure I'm interested either way, but... "Fine."

Alva squeals, but I already regret giving in. With a bit of luck, we'll see what Neleda's cooking up on our stakeout, and they'll leave me alone, satisfied that her deal's a pile of horseshit.

Nothing involving Neleda is good news.

CHAPTER THREE

OUT OF THE WATER

F inding the Rhodes's place is embarrassingly easy. Never fond of e-stone tablets, I don't own one, but Alva's more than happy to contribute hers to the cause. She types "Duke Rhodes address" in the search browser and the first entry gives us all of the information I could ever wish to know about my mother's new husband and then some. Salvar Rhodes, Duke of Elandheart in Ravelyn, married to one Neleda Stovrj-Rhodes. It even lists his blood type. Have these people ever heard of privacy?

Then I realize, he doesn't need it. He has guards and high towers to protect him from his enemies.

I read the address and head to the desk where we keep our maps.

"You realize we can look up the address on the globe, right?" Alva's always amused by my dislike of electronic devices. "It'll give us directions and everything."

Perhaps, but e-stones just hurt my brain.

I shoot her a glare and unfold the map of high town, looking for the unfamiliar area. Their avenues are so wide we could build five rows of undercity houses in between every of their blocks.

I spot the Stateside neighborhood at the north side of town, close to Royal Lane where the kings and queens of Xhera reside when they must visit Magnapolis.

I shake my head in a mixture of contempt and disbelief. "There's nowhere to hide. The next street's too far to see or hear much, and there's a large area separating the house from the pavement—a courtyard or a garden."

"We'll have to go at night. Sneak past the guards, open a window or a door." Khel's undeterred.

We've never attempted anything even remotely as risky before. What if we're caught? This idea seems worse and worse by the moment. Out loud, I say, "We can observe tomorrow, come back afterwards if we see an entry point."

They're ready first thing in the morning, which isn't like either of them. Alva's usually one to drag her feet until midday, and Khel doesn't show much enthusiasm about anything ever, but they're both thrilled by this mission. Me, not so much.

I wash and stare at the half-dozen outfits hanging next to my cot. In the lanes, no one would so much as raise an eyebrow at any of my clothes, but I'm at a loss as to what I'm supposed to wear uptown. My choices are jeans or cargo pants, and various compression tops.

Grandma Lyn sewed me a sundress every summer,

and I used to wear them when we had dinner once a week, but I keep those at her house. *My* house, I suppose. The four walls filled with books, hand-stitched clothes, and basic remedies brewed in her kitchen belong to me, now.

I put on white jeans and a green top. I consider what to do with the copper mane on top of my head. Most of the time, it's braided, then tucked under a hood. Brushing my hair's an endeavor I don't undertake lightly, given how much time and effort it takes, but I don't think an uptown woman would be caught dead with my bird's nest.

Khel takes pity on me. "Here, let me."

His nimble fingers braid half of the curls that reach to the middle of my back much faster than I would, and then twist it around my head like a crown. Some of my curls still fall loosely. Those, he brushes. The mirror reflects an insouciant woman whom I don't recognize —the kind of person who has half an hour to do something about her appearance every day. I'll never be that person, because when I have some free time, I prefer to spend it reading or making myself useful.

"I should convince you to cut that mess." Khel works as a hairdresser a couple of times per week. He silently, broodingly despairs of me. That also takes time, hence why I haven't yet. Plus, Grandma Lyn used to like my stupid hair. It reminded her of her younger days.

"I'm surprised you haven't asked yet." Alva keeps her hair pixie short, especially in the summer. "Ready?"

I'm not sure I'll ever be ready to spy into Neleda's

world, but I'm no coward, and if something has to be done, I'd much rather get it over with. So I nod.

- ·· -·· -··

Needless to say, my clothes are wrong. The other women here wear well-cut, expensive blouses, and trendy, colorful summer dresses. Khel throws his arm around my shoulders casually. To the casual onlooker, we could seem like a couple on a stroll, which makes me look less conspicuous. Alva's not a problem—as a petite, buxom blonde in a white dress, she's hardly ever glanced at twice.

It takes a while to get to the duke's property.

The tall house is well situated, directly opposite a green square—despite the blinding heat and the many water shortages in the undercity—with benches and a large fountain.

Supported by twelve columns, the red brick house boasts large windows and a tower with a sculpted lion on top.

I chuckle. I can't believe my mother is the mistress of this house—this *castle*.

As the map suggested, the gated property has a courtyard in the front and a garden in the back. We spot the guards patrolling in pairs outside, and the cameras aimed in every direction.

The wealth and opulence of the whole thing disgust me. What it takes to run this house for a single day could feed an entire neighborhood in the undercity for a month, if not more.

"I can't believe she lives here," Alva muses.

"We can't pull it off. Not even at night." There's no way to get into that house unseen.

"We *can*. You just don't want to. You don't have to come with us, but we're going in tonight," Alva declares.

My jaw ticks in annoyance. We've passed the house in a few more steps. I don't risk a backward glance, unmasked as I am, but I remember the setup well enough. My desires have little to do with the fact that this place is a fortress, protected by high gilded walls.

Even if we did find a way in, what could we find to incriminate Neleda? I don't expect her to have a folder on her desk labeled MY THREE-STEP EVIL PLAN.

"I'm the boss, remember?"

"I certainly do. I remember the day you won a race through the lanes against all of us, at *seventeen*, to earn the title when Manu retired. You lead us because you're faster, stronger, and smarter. If one person can get into this place unseen, it's you."

Even I don't realize how wrong she is.

CHAPTER FOUR
THE BEAST IN THE NIGHT

L e *droit du seigneur* is a brutish, outdated custom that should have long since been abolished, and most of the time, I pass on my right to fuck the women of my court on their wedding night. Not tonight.

The nimble beauty bouncing on my lap certainly knows how to please a man, but my only satisfaction is in seeing her groom's expression as I take his wife first.

I want Harl Greystone to watch me give more pleasure than he ever could to the poor girl. She's barely eighteen, and thrown at a man twice her age. It's the least I can do for her.

Harl turns greener at each of her elated screams. I'm not much for kissing, but I sit up and take her lips as she comes apart.

She falls to my chest and the court claps around us. Mira Meyerson's still completely dressed in her long white gown, only missing the panties dangling around one ankle. It wouldn't do to expose the lady's modesty to the entire court. She's a countess, after all.

I roll away from underneath her limp legs and lift my pants back into position.

Peers of the realm are quick to congratulate the bride and raise their goblets to toast. "May your fruit bless Mrs. Greystone's womb!"

I certainly hope not. I paid Callan Frejr, the best brewer I know, for a fresh contraceptive potion with tonight in mind. If it fails, I'll have the bastard hanged. I'm in need of an heir, but I'll be damned if my first brat belongs to the house of Greystone.

By law, as king of Ravelyn, I can taste any willing woman—or man—of age in my kingdom. Being taken by the king isn't considered adultery; it's technically a royal service, for which they are entitled a number of rewards.

A child born from such rutting would either belong to her birth family, or, should the woman be married, her husband's.

It's the first law I'll dismantle after I'm no longer shackled by the regents controlling me.

Harl is one such regent. He's spent the last fifteen years attempting to muzzle me. For a while, I needed their guidance, but I've been able to form my own thoughts for at least half a decade. They're pushing down my will in an effort to cling to power that never belonged to them.

My fucking Harl's young, pretty bride is the first event in a very long line of retributions I have in store for him. Some husbands are more than happy to throw their wives at me, but Harl's too proud, and too taken by the notion of his own self-importance for that. He doesn't want my favor. He doesn't think he needs it.

"Nicely done, Your Highness," Otto Nettlestein hisses between his teeth as he dogs my steps. "And the lady is quite pleasing. Would you consider making her part of your harem?"

I groan as we reach the entry hall of the Greystone townhouse.

I was sixteen when Otto first mentioned my building a harem, like my father and grandfather before me. I can't discount the appeal. It's safer, for one, and ensures a number of willing partners at my beck and call. But I have no time to cultivate relationships, not even with one person, let alone several. So, eight years later, I've yet to choose anyone.

"The girl's just married, Ot. Have some pity on poor Harl." My advisor snorts, aware of my disdain for the earl.

At least, some of it. He knows I resent how he and Salvar Rhodes strive to stifle my voice even now, when I'm only a season away from no longer needing a regent. What he doesn't realize is that I've hated the earl and the duke for far longer, and for an entirely different reason.

"If not her, then someone else. *Anyone* else," the short, stout man practically begs.

The son of a historian and a soldier, Otto is a true patriot. He lives and breathes Ravelyn, loves our kingdom more than anything and anyone. He'd betray his own mother for the good of the realm.

Which is why I trust him less than any of the snakes slithering at my feet. However, I like him more.

"Why don't you concern yourself with getting your own dick wet, rather than constantly worrying about mine?"

He's undeterred by my callousness. "You need an heir, sir."

I do. I am the last of the Devar line. Everyone else bearing my family's name is either buried six feet under or ashes carried away by the wind long ago. Since the foundation of Ravelyn, the Devars have ruled the frozen islands, and our patriarch ensured that only those who share his blood could sit on our throne.

What isn't common knowledge is that there are three other lines with Devar blood, thanks to that irksome, witless law about kings being entitled to anyone's pussy. The Greystones, the Adlers, and the Rhodeses. If I die childless, those three houses will tear the country apart to determine who will take my place.

What I don't need is a vulnerability, and a child would be just that, at least for the first decade or two. I can't afford such a distraction while surrounded by so many unseen, conniving enemies.

We walk out of the pleasantly fresh building, courtesy of air magik, and into the hellish furnace that is Magnapolis in the summer. The night is heavy and stuffy, and I rush to the vehicle bearing my coat of arms, a raven standing over the skull.

I live on Royal Lane, my home but a few short yards away from Stateside, and if it had been any other season, I would have gladly walked—to the annoyance of my guards—but I don't spend more time than strictly necessary outside in the heat. My skin feels like it's being slowly roasted over a pyre by the time I'm safely locked at the back of my hovercraft.

I half expect to see my face blotched and red in the reflection of the window, but I'm pale as usual, though my skin's glistening with a layer of sweat. Disgusted, I wipe it off with my handkerchief.

The craft barely hovers off the ground when I see a strange, out of place movement in the dark. I frown and squint through the window, staring at the back of the house across the street. I'm aware that the red brick townhouse belongs to the Rhodeses, although I've never stepped onto the property. There isn't much I'm not aware of about my enemies, and the duke of Elandheart certainly figures among them.

I catch another shift in the shadows, swift and just as peculiar.

"Wait."

Whatever it is, the thing moving high in the trees lining the property gates doesn't belong there. It's too large to be a squirrel, though it almost moves like one.

Then I see it. The shadow of a human figure running, then leaping from one of the branches of the trees lining the street to the metal fence. It jumps again, and reaches an oak tree in the back garden of the Rhodes townhouse.

I'll be damned. I've never seen a person move like that, with the grace and agility of a wild thing. It must be a demi of some description. Probably someone sent by the guild of assassins. Part of me wants to leave good old Rhodes to his fate, but I can't. I have too many questions, and my regent might find it hard to speak around a knife in his throat.

I get out of the craft, immediately followed by the two guards seated in the front compartment. I wave them back, gesturing for them to wait. They're used to such orders from me and they know better than to question it.

I cross the street.

At this time of night, the gate's closed, but before I have a chance to buzz the interphone, they open in front of me. The night guard must have recognized me through their camera.

The large green doors of the main house open as I cross the courtyard.

Salvar Rhodes stands in evening clothes, though his cravat's untied. A tall man appearing to approach his sunset years, with silver threading his dark hair and a walking stick, he's still quite handsome. Salvar's only in his third century, and the Devar blood in his veins should have kept him younger, but he aged like a common in the last few decades, thanks to a curse he never talks about.

The woman standing in a robe in front of him is stunning, I'll give him that. Perfect blonde ringlets and a pouty mouth made for taking cocks, she's any straight man's dream. So, that's his new wife, the common he saw fit to bring into my court. She's a pretty sight, and far too young for what he looks like now, which makes her an unapologetic gold-digging slut, and I can respect that.

"You'll excuse my intrusion," I tell her, rather than her husband. "I'd like to see your gardens."

The couple exchanges a bemused look, the duke recovering first. "Of course, Your Grace. I'll be glad to take you around."

"No need, old boy. I'll find my way just fine by myself."

I leave them to their bafflement, and walk to the back of the house, hoping I haven't missed the intriguing intruder.

I pass two guards who stare at me in confusion, before falling into a low bow. I could do without the interruption, but if there's one set of people I prefer to stay on the good side of, it's the Ravelyn military. "By the gods, what a shitty night. Aren't you sweltering in those cloaks?"

"No, sir, thank you, sir," the first barks.

He must be lying to avoid complaining in front of me. A pulse of familiar magik I feel around them tells me they're coldbloods, like me. We're native to the poles and fare badly under the mainland sun.

"The duke provided us with amulets," says the younger one, a boy barely out of his teens, with brown skin and silver-white curly hair. He pulls a charm dangling around his throat from under his shirt, holding it up at my eye level. "They help in the summer."

I'm reluctantly impressed. Spells of the sort cost a pretty penny, and I didn't expect Rhodes to be the kind of man who'd spend any of his resources on guards. "I should get one of those. Was today eventful?" I ask casually.

Both guards assure me that their shift was quiet and move to the courtyard, letting me enter the back garden.

I don't see anything strange myself, not in the trees, or behind the statues and lamp posts and benches. I might have believed I was entirely alone, if not for an awareness in the pit of my stomach.

We demis can usually feel each other at a distance, especially when the other person has a power of consequence. This feels different, however.

When I'm around the likes of Natheran Reiks, or some of the Frejr, my instincts tell me to watch a fellow predator. Right now, I'm not vigilant.

I'm playful.

Whatever this is, it's something else.

Something I want to catch.

CHAPTER FIVE

MIDSUMMER FROST

T he guard in the garden is seriously slacking off. Shouldn't he have moved to the front of the house by now? But no, he planted his ass right in front of the water fountain. He's clearly chilling out, enjoying the moisture in the air. I want to groan, but I can't risk any noise. Someone ought to rat him out to his boss.

My legs and the right arm I'm using to balance myself up on the branch of the old oak tree are starting to strain, and I'm dying to shift position, but if I move even a muscle, he might see me. My body's twisted at a strange angle that follows the lines of branches, but I can't keep it up forever.

Somewhat strangely, given my occupation, I'm not much for violence, though I can defend myself. Alva made sure to teach me a few dirty tricks, but my strength is stealth and efficiency, not combat. I *might* be able to take on one guard, with some luck, but he'll make noise and call the other two. And because we're uptown, there's a chance at least one of them might be enhanced, or worse, a demi.

If that's the case, I'm so, so screwed.

I'm as common as it gets, like most people from the undercity. There isn't so much as a drop of magik in my blood. Grandma Lyn was like me, but she managed to learn a bit of alchemy from whatever books she could afford to buy, and even got enhanced enough to be able to handle minor brewing. Balms that cure small ailments, like eczema or acne. If I'm very lucky, I'll eventually be able to do the same. Fancy combat magiks are something people like me can't even fathom.

The air's far less heavy uptown, but suddenly I shiver, almost cold. The eerie sensation isn't unwelcome after a month of sweating my tits off, but it's nevertheless strange on a summer night.

"One minute." I barely catch the guard's low, smooth timbre. "That's how long you have before you freeze to death, squirrel."

My next breath's a frozen cloud pluming out of my nose and mouth.

Shit.

"Come out and play. I promise I don't bite." The guard lies back on the bench, casual as ever.

I thought he was lazy. Turns out he's far worse.

In a heartbeat, the temperature drops considerably. Only a coldblood could have done that.

I remember Alva joking we could do with one of those on our team about a week ago, when the sun had been at its zenith. I'd agreed. Now, I'm biting my words back.

I assumed they'd be able to manage a small breeze or conjure up a bowl of ice. Not this devastation. Every plant in this garden is dying because he willed it so, effortlessly.

"Thirty seconds."

The fountain stops running, turning into ice, and the rose bushes frost over. In just a few instants, the pleasant garden has morphed into a frozen wonderland, gorgeous but no less deadly.

I could attempt to run back out, but demis tend to be athletic on top of everything else. Besides, thanks to Frost Man, I'm not sure the thinner branches could hold my weight now that they're frozen over.

"Ten. Nine. Eight."

I don't have much of a choice, so I stop procrastinating, and leap off the oak tree on unsteady legs, staying in a low crouch.

As my gaze lifts to his, I catch my first clear glance of the demigod who almost killed me.

Everything about him takes me aback. He doesn't look much like a guard. He's too young, too casual, and far too beautiful. Wild white-blond hair frames a sharp face with cheekbones cut like blades and a strong square jaw. The guards I spotted also wore black, hence my assumption, but his shirt is silky, with four buttons open, far less formal. "There you are."

Piercing blue eyes too bright in the darkness bore into mine and don't let go.

The man's dangerous, I can sense that. More dangerous than anything I've ever seen. The urge to run fights my instinct to stay still to avoid provoking the predator.

He pushes up his feet and strides toward me. "Not a squirrel, then. We have ourselves a vixen."

"Stay away." I'm glad to hear my voice come out firm, rather than shaking.

His footsteps are crisp against the frozen blades of grass he snaps beneath each step. "Now why would I do that, thief?"

He's right to call me that, and in most instances, if I were found on a random property in the middle of the night, it would be because I intend to steal something.

Today, the only thing I'm after is information.

"I'm not here to steal anything."

His laugh is low thunder that freezes my blood as surely as his devastating magik. "Mmkay."

"This is my mother's house," I finally croak.

The demi stills. His head tilts as he studies me slowly, from my folded legs to my messy hair.

I fully expect him to call me a liar. He caught me sneaking in. That's no daughter's behavior.

"Ah. You do look like the gold digger."

I should be offended on Neleda's behalf. Instead, I twist my lips at the corner, taking his words as an insult against me. "What sort of a guest insults his host's wife?"

"What sort of a daughter sneaks into the house in the dead of the night?" he counters.

I have no response.

"You truly don't know who I am, do you?"

I've never seen him in my life. I don't forget

anything or anyone, and I'd never forget someone who looks like *him*. Even if I could have failed to recall that face, that swagger, I would remember power like his. The kind that makes me feel like prey, immobile and afraid.

I know better than to show any of that. "Should I?"

I feel more comfortable crouched, poised to either run or fight, but now that he's so close, my diminutive height feels like a weakness, so I slowly get up.

I'm not tall by any stretch of imagination, but he makes me seem as dainty as Alva.

The stranger strolls to me, only stopping when we're close enough for me to smell his pine wood and cherry scent. From this distance, he's even more unsettlingly perfect. His pores are nonexistent; his natural glow makes him look airbrushed. I want to ask about his beauty routine, although there's a fair chance it involves drinking the blood of virgins.

"What hole have you crawled out of, if you can't recognize me?" He's clearly insulting me, but his tone remains light and pleasing.

"Sorry," I grit between my teeth. I can't recall ever being less sorry in my life. "I haven't listened to boy bands since I was ten. I'm sure you look great with eye shadow and tight pants, though." I'm guessing he's a celebrity of some persuasion.

He chuckles and bites his lip. "You know, some men find ignorance attractive. They love to think they can teach stupid pretty things like you." His eyes narrow. "Not my kink, sweetling."

I consider the likelihood of my bringing my knee to his junk before he can freeze me to death.

Just as I decide to give it a go, my mother rushes out of her house. "Helyn? Helyn, is that you?" She comes to a stop in the middle of her frozen garden, surveying the damage.

Shit. I'm doubly caught. I knew the mission was a wash the moment this guy interfered, but I'd hoped to sneak away. Now she's seen me here.

My mind races, considering my options.

The stranger ignores her, keeping his burning blue eyes locked on me. "I'll see you at court," he finally says, turning on his heels and leaving me alone with Neleda.

Her gaze follows the boy until he's out of view, then flies back to me. "By the gods!" she practically yells, eyes wide. "What were you doing alone with the king? Is he courting you, Helyn? He has no wife, and not even a harem, you know. If he were to consider you, you'd have a shot at the crown!" I've never seen her this excited, not even when she was daydreaming about pimping me out to a brothel. I guess a king is a step up.

I tune her out, feeling like the ignorant, stupid girl the coldblood accused me of being.

Twenty-something, blond, powerful, alone in the garden of a duke of Ravelyn. I really should have known who he was. I've seen portraits of him, painted by Sir Mordov and Theleva Sand. Plenty of coins sporting his regal profile have slid between my fingers.

I was just in the presence of Zale Devar, king of Ravelyn.

At least I didn't knee his junk.

CHAPTER SIX

THE LEISURE OF KINGS

I'm back in the delightfully crisp northern air before dawn. Ravelyn has two seasons: night and day. Our land remains covered in snow throughout the year, especially high up in the mountains at the Whyte Fort.

I was scheduled to stay in Magnapolis for two days, but the beauty of being king is that I occasionally boast the luxury of following my whims. None of my meetings are crucial. Otto will bitch, but I can reschedule. I'll be in the city the entire fall and half of winter—my treaty negotiations with the trade guild can wait until then.

As soon as she was aware of my presence, the queen of Flaur asked me for tea, which is another word for a parade of long skirts and tight corsets. I'm pleased to escape that invitation. She has yet to abandon the notion of throwing one of her nieces at me, futile as her attempts are. I know better than to mix my blood with mainlanders. Since the days of Tryn Devar, the first of our kings, the throne has passed to coldbloods, and I'll see that the tradition continues. To ensure my heir's blood remains pure, I can either breed with another coldblood or a common, and I'll never debase myself as to choose a magikless, short-lived mortal fools. We're not even the same species. Their ancestors trace back to evolved monkeys, mine are major gods.

Escaping Aude Briar's matchmaking wasn't the main goal of my returning home early, but it certainly doesn't hurt. I left because I couldn't bear to remain in Magnapolis. I underestimated my dislike for the stench of the international city, and for the blinding heat. And, I'm loath to admit it, but I also was acutely ruffled by the girl in the tree.

I didn't lie when I said she looked like the duke's shiny new trophy wife. They have the same heart-shaped face, small turned-up nose, and bright green eyes. For all that, they *feel* like opposites. The animalistic awareness I have for all living creatures doesn't so much as register with most commons, and I barely noticed the mother. The daughter? I felt her even before I saw her.

No common should have alerted my senses, even as a blip.

Their differences don't stop at their auras. One has perfectly coiffed blonde ringlets and the other sports a red bird's nest. Where the duchess wore a skimpy, silky robe that made no secret of the shape of her ample chest, the vixen was dressed like one of my warriors, in well-worn, form-fitting fighting gear not unlike the ones I wear for training. The only bit of skin I could glimpse other than her face were her arms, not as tanned as they should have been for someone who lives in the city. That tells me she doesn't go out much during the day. I wonder what she does with her time. I wonder her name. I think her mother said it. What was it again?

I shouldn't care. She's a common thorn, elevated only because her mother spread her milky thighs to secure a match well beyond her station.

"Your Grace." As my supplicant curtsies, I don't miss how she thrusts her breasts forward to give me a view of her deep neckline. I want to grimace at the common slut, but she's not worth the backlash. "With your leave, I'd like to ask for my husband's land to remain in my hands now that he's dead."

I shift on the infernal black stone throne inscribed with ancient runes. By the seven hells, why do they keep removing my cushions?

"Who is supposed to inherit?" I ask, bored and frustrated.

I'm tired of handling stupid requests such as these. The only cases of note are overseen by my regents.

"A cousin of my husband's. My Henry is barely cold in his grave and Nick already sent me a notice to vacate the house." She sniffles and bats her lashes. "I have nowhere to go."

I pride myself on reading people well, and this woman is full of shit. I don't know whether she killed said husband or just married him for his fortune, but

she's far from sorrowful. I'd only have to crook a finger
and she'd hop on the throne and ride me.

Grieving or not, if she put up with the man, she's
entitled to compensation for it, according to the laws of
my land. Entailed territories are a tricky business,
though. "Your file," I request.

She rushes forward to hand me the folder in her
grasp, but before she approaches the dais of the throne
room, I extend my palm and it flies out of her fingers.

I'd rather keep my distance from the plebe.

I scan through the document, finding exactly what
I expect. She's indeed a common. She's dyed her hair
white and painted her face with paler colors, but no
subterfuge can hide the heat of her flesh or the blush
under her skin. At twenty-six, she wedded an eighty-
seven-year-old minor demi who aged as fast as
commons. The guy died of a heart attack. I snort,
leering at his salacious wife. I bet she made sure to work
his aging heart extra hard. As lucky old Henry was a
baronet, his land is linked to the title, and should
indeed go down to the next male in his family, one
Nicholas Turret.

Henry, like many heirs of once relevant families,
gambled away his fortune and sold whatever land he
had except for the main house to settle his debts. That's
the quandary—he didn't have anything to leave his
wife, and she deserves some sort of compensation for
taking the limp dick for three years. On the other hand,
it's hardly Nicholas's fault if she didn't check the
financials before tying herself to a losing horse.

"Nothing can be done about the baronetcy." I sigh,

my disgust tinged with a sliver of pity. Common or highborn, I am fair to all my subjects. "The crown will relocate you—you'll have a comfortable house and a stipend for seven years. I suggest you have your affairs in order by the end of it. Next."

My morning is filled with local disputes, land drama, and the occasional backstabbing quarrel; I pardoned the wife who found her husband in bed with her brother and killed them both, if only because she's the most entertainment I've had all day. By lunchtime, I haven't yet buried a bullet in my skull, so I head over to the sparring ring and I work out some of my frustration with my fists.

I don't reflect on anything concerning the redhead at any point all day, because I don't let myself.

She's just common.

CHAPTER SEVEN

IN THE WOLF'S DEN

The man on the other side of the dining room table looks unsettlingly normal.

Dressed in a casual shirt and beige slacks, he eats his eggs and bacon with gusto, smiling at me under his salt-and-pepper mustache. "Don't you love mainland food?" He tears through a crusty bread roll and munches it happily.

"I haven't ever had any other food," I reply, still dumbfounded.

Last night, after the freaking *king* left, Neleda rushed me into the house, introduced me to her husband and quickly ushered me into a room before I could make a run for it.

I opted to stay. I can't get the answers I need unless I'm inside the house, and after yesterday, I'm convinced being a guest and snooping is a lot safer than attempting to break in. The design of the house makes it almost impossible to get inside without being seen. The armed guards deterred me to start with—I wouldn't have risked an attempt if Khel and Alva hadn't been so insistent—but I was almost frozen to death. I'm not trying that again.

I paced inside the luxurious pink and silver princess room all night, not even taking advantage of the plush canopy bed. In the morning, a servant knocked and offered me a change of clothes I declined, and a toothbrush I accepted, before leading me to the family dining room—as opposed to the less intimate banquet hall we passed on the way.

And now I'm having breakfast with a duke and, even more surprising, my mother.

"Helyn is a city girl at heart. She hasn't travelled," Neleda answers for me.

My jaw tightens in annoyance. How dare she presume to be aware of where I have and haven't travelled? I could have sailed around Xhera twice for all she knows.

"Well, Helyn, Ravelyn is a kingdom made of two islands, so naturally, we eat a lot of fish," the duke explains. "The temperature is harsh on both parts of the country, so we can't grow many crops. Trade has changed things in the last few hundred years, as it does, but in the old days, Ravelyn's food mostly consisted of dried or frozen meats and grilled fish. We get flour and produce now, but our cooks aren't quite sure what to do with it yet."

I find his friendly, open demeanor suspicious. He's a noble of high rank—what's more, a demi—and he's as chatty and jolly as Old Pop Bill down the lane.

The man's a little old for Neleda, but he's attractive

enough for a fifty-something year old, and they make a pretty picture together. The family dining room's too rich for my blood, as are the silver cutlery and porcelain dishes, but the food on my plate's no different than what Grandma Lyn cooked for me when we could afford bacon.

I know there's a trick somewhere. I just can't pinpoint which part.

"I don't eat fish often," I offer. The man's friendliness makes it almost impossible not to be polite, despite the freakish circumstances. "But I love it."

He seems to take that as a personal compliment. "You'll enjoy our food, then. We prepare fish a thousand different ways, all of them delicious." He sighs. "Though I admit, it gets tiring after three centuries."

"You're three centuries old?" And here I thought he looked a little gray. The man's in *great* shape for his age.

"Three hundred and twelve next winter." He grins, piling his plate with pancakes. "How about you? Your mother said you're eighteen?"

Figures she doesn't remember when she gave birth. "I'm nineteen. Probably a baby to your eyes."

"Not really. After a while, a grown woman is a grown woman." He shrugs. "So, tell me about yourself, Helyn. Pancake?"

I shake my head. I ate more for breakfast than I normally eat in an entire day. "Nothing much to say. I'm your typical girl from the undercity."

"Bah!" The duke drowns his pancake in syrup. "No

one's typical, and everyone has a story. Your mother tells me you have a good memory, yes?"

My eyes cut to Neleda. Sitting at the head of the table, she's barely eaten a thing, while we pigged out to either side of her.

I didn't know she was aware of that. "Yeah. I don't forget stuff."

"You know, I know people who paid witches their weight in gold for that skill."

I shrug both shoulders, not particularly proud of something I haven't earned or practiced. My brain just works that way.

"You're humble." He turns to Neleda and smiles at her teasingly. "Are you sure she's your daughter?"

"Hardly." Neleda attempts to return his smile, but it drops fast. "I didn't raise Helyn, my mother did. She's more of an estranged sister, if anything."

So she was honest to her husband about her role in my life—or lack thereof.

The duke puts a steadying hand on my mother's lap, comforting her. I'm more and more baffled by the situation I walked into.

"Well, maybe we can remedy that, hm? At least the estranged bit." He looks between us. "Listen, Helyn, you're wary, and I get it. Nel told me everything she did, and didn't, do to you. It was shitty, but we're going to fix it."

I stare at him for a good while before chuckling. "If only saying it would make it so, sir."

"Call me Salvar—Sal, if you prefer. And it is so. You're my wife's daughter. The curse that ages me also prevents me from having children, and there's no way of breaking it, so as of six months ago, you're my heir, whether you like it or not." He throws his hands up in the air in a theatrical gesture. "It's done."

What the hell? "Just like that, huh?"

"Just like that." He sets his knife and fork to the side and wipes his mouth. "It's sealed and filed already. You can return to the undercity and carry on with your life, you'll still be a lady of Ravelyn now, and duchess of Elandheart after our deaths."

I'm too stunned to even think of an answer. Me, a duchess? And of somewhere I hadn't even heard of two days ago. It makes no sense whatsoever.

The duke is all business now. "Here's what I propose: the occasional dinner to make your mother happy, some court appearance to pave your future, and in your free time..." He glances at his wife. "Whatever you like. Your mother said you might be interested in school, yes? I went to Five myself, and I'd be happy to recommend you for admittance. You might have to study a little to pass the entry test, but I'll finance your studies if you wish to attend."

This offer comes with strings. He wants me to play the dutiful daughter to a snake I'd rather not see again. But the benefits...

I could get an education. At *Five*. The Five Kingdoms' Superior University, where the rich, the titled, and the crowned send their heirs. And maybe I could make a difference, like Alva said. After hearing all that, I need a moment to think.

"In my experience," I say carefully, "if something sounds too good to be true, it generally is."

"Ha!" He nods his head. "I like her, Nel. She says it like it is."

"Like I said, I didn't raise her." Neleda does manage a smile now.

"Well, Helyn, it might seem like only good things when I lay it out to you like this, but the truth? It's going to be a hard road, kid. Ravelyn is elitist and the court is a lion's den. They don't accept Nel, and they won't accept you. Not for a good long while. And if you choose to go to Five?" He winces. "In my days, common kids were treated like shit. I doubt it's changed much."

I don't understand this man's logic. "Then why did you choose a common wife?"

"I didn't choose a common wife, I chose Neleda." He takes her hand. "She's not good. She's not even nice. I'm not the kind of man who enjoys good or nice."

Now that's more like what I expect of a noble demi. "So, if you're a ruthless asshole like my mother, why exactly should I believe a word you're saying to me?"

"Because I love this woman, and you're her daughter, which makes you part of my family."

I'm growing annoyed and impatient. "Bullshit." I've never been *family* to Neleda. Just someone she could use.

"How about you follow me?" The duke stands, and so does my mother. "And by the by, I enjoy a bit of colorful language as much as the next man, but I suggest you hold your tongue at court. Our young king doesn't suffer disrespect."

An image of the man in the garden, just as he was when he stood barely two feet away last night, flashes in my mind and I curse my stupid memory. He made me uncomfortable then, and I'm even more bothered now, knowing who he is.

Our young king doesn't suffer disrespect.

I'll bet. With those cold blues eyes, I'd be surprised if he tolerates *anything* but complete submission.

I hesitate when I get up, considering making a hasty retreat via the window. I mistrust everything out of Salvar Rhodes's mouth, if only because he married my mother. Carefully, I trail his steps, watching for an exit at every turn. Windows, unguarded doors.

I want to escape, but if I leave without finding concrete proof that he's talking out of his ass, Alva's going to spit in my stew for a month straight.

We walk through white stone halls and corridors until we reach a vast, oddly untidy hardwood study.

The duke circles an oval table where a map of Xhera is spread, marked with several hand-carved figures—castles and boats, sigils and vehicles. I look at the map in wonder, noticing each handwritten note: UNSTABLE, over the court of Flaur, and HIDDEN at the capital of Dorath. Even smaller territories merit mentions here.

If we were at war, I'd think this was a strategic map, meant for planning schemes to destabilize each realm. There hasn't been an open inter-kingdom conflict since the Dark War and the founding of Magnapolis, the city of the five kingdoms, so he must keep the information for another reason. Still, it seems seriously sensitive. Salvar knows I'll remember everything I see here, but he doesn't seem bothered one way or another. He makes for his desk, unlocks it with a key at his belt, and pulls a blue leatherbound volume.

He pages it and slides it along the large desk. "Go on, take a look."

Still highly skeptical, I do take a peek, too curious to help myself.

The page he stopped at lists names, with dates of birth and information. At the top, a decorative sigil features the name of his duchy: Elandheart.

I scan past the list of unfamiliar names, until the very end. The last line reads: *Salvar Rhodes, born nones of Imboloc year 1107, married to Neleda Stovrj, born ides of Litha year 1384. Heir: Helyn Stovrj, born nones of Samhain 1400.*

"What's this?" My voice is barely over a whisper.

"The latest version of the peerage, printed three months ago. Check it out at any bookstore if you want to be sure it's real."

My name is in the peerage, along with my date of birth. I was wrong, then: my mother knew exactly when I was born. Though the words are right before my eyes, I can't wrap my head around it.

"Sometimes good things *can* happen to you, Helyn," my mother says.

I don't believe a word she says, this least of all, but I'm starting to see that the only way I can spring their trap is by joining the game.

I can stay the fuck away, or I can play the players and take whatever I can get my hands on in the process.

This is a job. Maybe the largest job ever to come my way. I'm going to take from the rich, privileged assholes ruling this world, to redistribute the resources in my city.

Money, resources, influence. I'll claim everything I can and leave with my head high when the time comes.

If I play my cards right, this could even come with a side dish of vengeance against the woman who's wronged me in so many ways.

"All right, I'm in."

CHAPTER EIGHT

ON ANOTHER PATH

T tug at the hem of my smart blouse, the lace collar as comfortable as a shackle around my neck.

The girl parking her two-seater speeder between a hovercraft and an antique racecar looks nothing like me. In white thigh-high socks, leather loafers, and a gray pleated skirt, she almost blends in with the crowd walking away from the parking lot toward the grandiose entrance of Five.

I got in. In fact, my stepfather let me know that my entrance exam grades were so high they bumped me up to the last year of undergrad, despite my only having a grade school diploma. So long as I pass all the required tests by the end of the year, they'll give me a bachelor's, and I can start working on a master's next year.

The fact that on paper my name reads Stovrj-Rhodes might have something to do with that.

Last season, I was a street rat. Now I'm a lady of Ravelyn. The clothes, the car, and the dorm suite that come with it itch like poison ivy. It almost feels like I've become everything I despise.

Khel and Alva are delighted with the turn of events. Me, not so much.

A lump sum so high I nearly fainted my first time seeing it gets deposited into a new account in my name every four weeks. "For expenses," according to the duke. I funnel most of it straight through to Alva. If this farce continues for a whole year, I'll have given over a hundred thousand golds to those in need in the undercity. I don't need it—my meals are covered by my dorm fee, and my mother bought me an entire new wardrobe, along with electronic devices I never use and the stupid speeder that could house and feed a hundred orphan until they come of age.

"Lady Helyn!" A perfectly poised, smiling woman dressed in a formal black and green suit approaches.

I grit my teeth, unreasonably irritated by the stupid title. "It is I."

It is I. What in the seven purgatories is happening to me?

"I'm your attaché, Madeline Highgrove." She forces the fakest smile I've ever seen. "At your service."

My attaché looks like she's sucking on a lemon, and would rather pry off her manicured nails than stand too close to me.

"No, thanks. Services entirely unnecessary."

She drops the smile, thank the gods. "Ma'am, I was selected by Lord Rhodes himself."

And I don't doubt she was perfectly charming to my stepfather when he picked her.

"I don't need anyone licking my boots, Madeline." Her, least of all. "I'll manage."

Her mouth pinches into one thin line. "You're to be a duchess. Tradition demands…"

"I'll clear it with Sal, don't worry. I won't let him know you hated my guts at first sight, no doubt because I'm common." I might have to retract my claws and pretend I'm part of this world, but I'll be damned if I let anyone attempt to make me feel lesser.

She blanches. "It's a pleasure to serve the house of Rhodes. For generations, my family has—"

"And you can keep being a good little servant. Just not to me." I leave her standing on the sidewalk, close to the speeder, stunned.

Maybe she believed I'd fall over, grateful and dazzled to have a demi at my beck and call. Now she knows better.

I don't miss a few curious glances from the surrounding throng of students walking into the university. Our exchange has caught some attention, which wasn't my goal, but I doubt the fact that the house of Rhodes gained a common as its heir is a secret.

I direct my attention to the map of the campus that arrived along with my acceptance. The main building, as majestic as one would expect the old royal keep of Vanemir to be, stands right before my eyes, in its dark, sculpted, and gilded glory.

Magnapolis is built between Flaur, Vanemir, and Anderkan, as proof of the international cooperation the city represents. The ancient castle was donated to create this school, on Vanemir ground, when the royal family decided to transport their court north, closer to the Darklands.

The dorms are situated in the left wing, an addition built much later, as the simpler, wide white stone architecture attests. The modern amenities make it much more convenient, so the royal family moved there for a few hundred years, before moving north and giving the castle away. And now, it's my dorm.

The five-story building is arranged like most modern constructions: the rooms are larger on the lower floors and get smaller and smaller as you go up. The top floor used to house servants. Downstairs, the greater halls, like the throne rooms, were turned into dining rooms, guard barracks, and study halls. The second floor, where greater political meetings used to take place, is harboring three occupants: two princes and one princess.

My suite is on the third floor. The kings and queens of Vanemir used to sleep there. My room, study, and bathroom are about the size of two lanes of the undercity put together. It's ridiculous.

Since ridiculous is my new normal, I just pick up the books I ordered to be delivered directly to the house, and head out to meet my guidance counselor.

"Your schedule isn't going to be easy, Lady Rhodes."

"Hel," I correct out of habit. "You can drop the lady."

The Rhodes, I can get used to. I've never been one to go by my family name, so Stovrj doesn't mean much to me. The "lady" bit, however...

"Ms. Rhodes," the small, skinny man rewords. "You'll have a test every other week in the first semester to cover your first and second years, and while things do slow down afterwards, it's only because the curricula of the last two years are considerably more demanding. You'll still attend all fourth-year classes, and it is up to you to catch up in order to pass your tests. The instructors will be at your disposal to answer questions, but I won't lie." He shakes his head. "I don't know one student who's had this kind of workload in the past."

He doesn't trust I can do it. I grin. "Understood. Can I have my curricula now?"

The man hesitates, a hand on the brown folder between us on his glass desk. "If you don't manage to test out of all of your courses, we can review your schedule. It's not a problem. Just reach out and we can make the timetable more manageable."

I've never heard anyone as condescending. I know right there and then that I'll manage his hellish schedule, if only out of spite.

CHAPTER NINE

A DIFFERENT KIND OF SPELL

T urns out, if morphing lead into gold isn't common practice, it's likely because the process is annoyingly lengthy and boring as all purgatories.

I did wonder why the poor didn't bother to learn the craft. Given the fact that it's alchemy rather than magik, they could buy pounds of lead for cheap and all their troubles would be over. Now I know better. What peasant has a full five hours to spare, staring at a mostly empty bowl of spider legs in order to sharpen the container? And it's just step one in a long list. I have all the time in the world, and I'm struggling to keep my focus on the assignment after only one hour.

We have a two-day session to get the assignment done, and I can already tell I'll walk out of this room with a pounding headache.

I don't have many courses this semester, and most of them are hands-on, practical lessons such as this one. The only reason why I'm back at Five is to maintain the illusion of normalcy. In a few weeks—fifteen, to be exact—I will turn twenty-five, and come into my reign without need of a regent. If I can manage to write my second thesis before then, all the better. If I don't, I suppose I'll have to be satisfied with being the first Ravelyn king to hold a master's. The rest of my lineage didn't bother to go past a bachelor's degree, but studying does entertain me. After the crown is truly mine, I'll have other concerns.

"I'm sorry I'm late, Mr. Heffur."

All of my attention immediately leaves the chalice and zeroes in on the girl striding into my metamorphosis class. There goes my hour of work. I'll have to start again from scratch.

It takes me far too long to compute what I'm looking at. The preppy young woman dressed in a coordinating ensemble—beige skirt and pink cardigan over a white shirt—looks nothing like the vixen in the duke's garden. The only thing they have in common is the uncontrollable bird's nest atop the heart-shaped face.

"Ah, yes, Lady Rhodes." The professor doesn't glance up from the rim of his own goblet.

Lady? Fucking lady.

"I was told you had a conflict in your schedule—astrology before my class, right? Come in, come in. We only just started."

Instead of returning to my work, I watch her walk to the empty seat no one ever wants, front and center, right in front of Heffur. Her hair bounces happily with each of her steps. She should look ridiculous, but as put together as she is right now, the wild curls seem to be a purposeful style.

She pulls out everything on the list of required ingredients from a light blue satchel. The first thing I note is that while a metal goblet is required, hers has a glass bowl, though the rim is silver.

"You've prepped already." The teacher seems both surprised and impressed.

"I knew I'd be late. Is that all right, sir?"

She sounds respectful and subservient. I want to puke.

"Of course..." Heffur hesitates. "You sharpened the container yourself, yes? The spell won't work for you otherwise."

From my vantage point close to the window and three rows back, I see her jaw tick, but she hides her annoyance under perkiness. "Yep. I did it while we waited for the lunar eclipse, sir. I used a magnifying glass to cut down the time. That's allowed, right?"

At that, the teacher does finally drag his gaze away from his spell, and gapes at her. "My lady, that's a dangerous practice. Done wrong, you could burn your eyes out or worse."

"I researched it, sir." She's all smiles. "And it worked out."

The professor blinks slowly. "Well, everyone, I was going to mention the custom later, but as Lady Rhodes has brought it to our attention, I will tell you about intense sharpening. With a magnifying glass, one can expedite our current spell, but at great personal risk: should you break your concentration for even an instant, the goblet will reflect the intensity of your focus right back at you, which can cause harm or even, in extreme cases, death. I will now demonstrate the practice, and those who wish to attempt it may. I strongly advise against it, however."

"How much time is it going to save?" I ask, seriously annoyed he's never said a word about it before.

Part of my irritation stems from the fact that the vixen knew about it and I didn't.

"Intense sharpening cuts down the duration to one tenth of the necessary time, so in this case, about thirty minutes."

Seriously? He wasted an hour of my life. Heffur is lucky he's from Dorath. If he was one of my citizens, I would have had him thrown in a dark dungeon for a whole week for the offense. "I'll need a magnifying glass."

"Your Grace, I must beg you to choose the safer path. I can't have you come to any harm in my class."

I grit my teeth. "Are you suggesting I can't manage something the foxy teacher's pet here did?"

"Not at all, not at all." The teacher cleans the rim of his half-moon glasses with a cloth he then uses to dab his brow. "But the risk..."

Never mind where he's from. I'll skin him alive either way if he doesn't shut his hole.

The redheaded vixen rifles through her bag and retrieves a leather pouch. "Here, you can use mine."

She holds it up in the air, expecting me to go to her.

My fingers dig into the side of my desk, cool anger rising to the surface in waves at everything about this situation: the teacher's insolence, this common girl treating me like she's my equal.

I get to my feet and start to walk, pausing by her desk. I ignore the tool bag still in her hand. "Who do you think you are?"

Her mouth parts but she has the wits to not attempt an answer.

"Your mother may have spread her thighs to one of my subjects, but I am your king. Not your friend, not your peer. You don't get to talk to me unless I say so. Understood?"

I catch the way her skin reddens, an angry blush starting at the throat and covering almost all of her face. I wonder how far it extends under the clothes she chose to hide herself, to pretend she's one of us.

I don't move, demanding an answer.

"What? I thought I wasn't supposed to speak."

That mouth—and that attitude—is going to get her into so much trouble.

I snort on my way out of the study hall.

She chose her fate. When the chips fall, she can't say I didn't warn her.

CHAPTER TEN
AGAINST THE CURRENT

T he next several weeks are amazing and terrible
all at once.

I can't say I miss the constant stress I was
under in the lanes, but I am restless in this new role of
mine.

I don't have to roam the rooftops in search of a
mark, risking my neck to steal what I can to ensure my
neighborhood survives. I don't even have to feel guilty
about not being out there, because the amount of
money I'm giving Alva helps the undercity far more
than my heists ever could.

I soak in every bit of information I can get, and I
love the person I am becoming. Each new book
transforms me, broadening my understanding of the
world, making me feel powerful. The next time I see
someone suffer from a fever, I know what weed to
collect in the streets to ease their discomfort. Instead of
staring in helpless horror when someone is about to die
of sepsis, I know how to make a salve almost as

efficaceous as a witch's spell. There's a stone from Dorath that, if activated on a blood moon, will warm the hearth of one's home for an entire year. If I can get my hands on some, and distribute them to the households at risk, it might save hundreds, if not thousands of people in the harsh winter.

I know so much more than I did before summer, and it's not even Lughnasadh.

Five itself is a quandary. The duke did warn me: I am not welcome here. I never was from the start, but the king of Ravelyn ensured that I remained a pariah.

I'm dressed the part, and I'm doing okay in all of my classes. More than okay. In the last six weeks, I've passed three tests. The results of the first two were straight As, and the third hasn't yet been confirmed, but I'm fairly certain I answered all the questions accurately. For all that, I'm a freak. Everyone hates me. Because *he* decided I was to be hated.

My first interaction with the king of Ravelyn left a cold, dangerous impression. He would have killed me without hesitation if I hadn't obeyed him in the garden. Still, I tried to be nice when I met him again. What a monumental failure.

The alchemy study group was an advanced lab placement with less than a dozen students, yet the next day everyone had heard of our exchange. Suddenly, people either called me Foxy or Vixen. I am accused of sucking up to—or downright sucking—teachers for my grades, although I'm working my ass off. The knowledge that my mother married into money hadn't bothered anyone before, but all of a sudden, I was reminded at every corner that Neleda's only worthwhile attribute was between her legs. Some painted, poised woman with impossibly high heels asked me whether my new daddy put me to bed and sang me a lullaby. The sickening implication made me want to throw punches, but I refrained.

I've barely seen the king in the four weeks since the alchemy group, but every insult, every snarl reminds me of him. His presence is pervasive. My only space, the only place he hasn't yet infected, is the library.

I do occasionally encounter a bitchy sycophant, but I'm too busy to pay attention. Besides, the cavernous room has so many alcoves and private spaces between its columns and rows of dusty old volumes, it's not hard to disappear when I don't want to be seen.

If someone had told me I could be even remotely comfortable anywhere in this opulent world, I wouldn't have believed it, but the library has become my sanctum. I feel at home there, more than I did in the underground den I shared with Khel and Alva.

As my counselor pointed out, I don't have to attend many classes this term. I'm given the subjects of my courses and an extensive list of reading materials. I go to my teachers when there's a specific point I need to understand, but usually, I only turn up to class when there's a practical lab.

Most of the research happens in the tower of magiks, although alchemy barely qualifies as one of the four fundamental types of magiks: witchcraft, metamorphosis, summoning, and innate magik.

As no magiks need be called upon, alchemy is closer

to physics and chemistry than anything else, though it does involve a degree of metamorphosis, and has historically been considered a type of craft. It is the craft of the erudite; it takes extensive knowledge in hundreds of subjects to manage the simplest task through science rather than magik.

My first experiment, turning lead to gold, impressive though it was, was also the least complex. During our last session, we infused a goblet with essence of life, which means that anyone who drank from said cup would find all of their ailments cured. It took an entire week, and the spell will only work once.

Thankfully, the high and mighty pain in the ass didn't attend that session. I can't imagine being locked in a small room with him for days on hand. I'd end up attempting murder, and getting my ass frozen to death in the process.

I'm surprised the king deigns to take the course at all, when alchemy is the craft of commons.

I expect him to be absent again, but when I enter the circular laboratory on Luprday, Zale Devar is seated right where he was the first lab: fourth row, close to the window. His frigid blue eyes set on me the moment I enter.

I wish I didn't gulp. I wish my instincts didn't scream at me, demanding I turn right back out of the room.

I fight myself, and rush to my seat.

There are only seven students today. Alchemy isn't what one would call popular. Our graying teacher isn't here yet, so I set out to display the long list of required ingredients around my work space, pretending I'm not shivering and feeling his gaze at my back.

I don't know what he has against me, but his hatred is a palpable, harrowing, icy flame. It can't just because I'm not a demi—there are plenty of other common attendees at Five. Granted, I suppose he could be a major dick to them, too.

I release a breath when Mr. Heffur walks in, carrying a heavy tray behind him. "Oh, good, good, you're all here!"

Though he's shorter than Alva and thin as a wraith, he effortlessly lugs what looks like thirty stones of food: ripe apples, heaps of berries, and golden loaves of bread. There's enough sustenance to feed a small army.

"As you know, we're approaching the celebration of Lughnsadh—or Lammas." He inclines his head toward the voluptuous, ochre-skinned beauty at the back. I think she's from Dorath, one of the countries that still uses the old tongue. "Now, Lammas is primarily a harvest festival, but what *is* a harvest? One might reap fruits and grain, of course. Can think of anything else?"

My hand shots up in the air.

"Let the rest of the class think, hm?" His gaze sweeps the space. "Anyone else?" No one volunteers, so the professor sighs. "Lady Rhodes?"

"Souls. The ancients used to get behind doors and seal every window on Lammas because hungry spirits roamed Xhera in search of unprotected souls."

"Your ancients, maybe." I don't have to turn to know who that low timbre belongs to. "Not mine."

The rest of the room chuckles. He's right: those

who did hide on Lammas were commons. The gods and their descendants didn't have much to fear from eldritch spirits.

"Right on both accounts, my lady and Your Grace." The teacher is either tone deaf, or choosing to ignore the animosity. "Mortals did indeed have much to fear on Lammas before the wilder things of this world were locked beyond the eternal gates. And the immortals did something quite different. Any idea what?"

Participation isn't our group's strongest suit, and for once, I am at a loss. I have no clue what the gods were up to. Immortals aren't my concern. I don't ignore texts about them if I happen to find some, but I don't go looking for information.

"I'll give you a clue. To this day, the demis still feel similar needs."

The class chuckles again, this time, not at my expense. I find it more uncomfortable because I'm left out of the loop.

Mr. Heffur is quick to enlighten me. "All festivals tend to encourage the baser instincts, but Lammas doesn't simply increase the urge to copulate. It is a celebration of reaping, and so among the eight celebrations in the wheel of the year, it is the one that's most associated with reproduction. Over half of the births happen after Ostara because many pregnancies start on Lammas."

Oh.

"So, to mark the occasion, we're going to create an eternal youth potion. These brews have to be drunk every year on Lammas, and will ensure you won't physically age for one year." The teacher chuckles. "Not useful to you, Your Grace, but the rest of us could use a little pick-me-up."

I can't help glancing behind me. The king casually reclines on his chair, relaxed as ever.

"The price is that you will not be able to conceive a child during that year."

I'm nineteen, and hardly interested in children, but I also don't see the point in stopping my aging right now. That said, I can't deny I'm curious to see the process, and who knows? It might come in handy in a decade or two.

I get to work.

CHAPTER ELEVEN
THE SIREN'S SONG

Ninety-seven hours later, I'm dead on my feet. The walls of the stuffy alchemy lab have never felt more constricting. We've had longer experiments, but none so precise or dizzying. A cloud of thick smoke has been our companion at all times.

There are cots prepared in an adjacent room to catch a few naps at appropriate stages during long labs like this one, but I'm not about to close my eyes on enemy territory. I'd like to think the teacher's presence would prevent the asshole king and his posse from messing with me, but I don't intend to take chances.

Unlike our teacher and some of the other students, Devar didn't take a break either. I would have noticed, and daydreamed about pouring itching powder all over him as he lay unconscious.

After all this time, I've brewed the most disgusting stew ever created, and simmered it down into a flask's worth of putrid, pungent concoction.

Drinking this potion is so not worth an extra year of youth. I can't imagine making myself guzzle that crap down to erase a few wrinkles.

"Flawless as usual, Lady Rhodes," Mr. Heffur croons, after checking a drop of my work. "I don't have one single comment."

He offers me a sunny smile, and strolls to the back of the class.

Grinning at the praise, I get to my feet and start to gather my instruments to bring them to the nearby sink for a thorough wash. I'm not putting any of the things I used back in my fancy bag.

"Hm."

Hearing a distinct note of disapproval, I'm curious enough to raise my head and glance at our teacher.

"Did you boil the toad for seven minutes, Ms. Lawrence?"

The charming Dorathian girl frowns, visibly trying to recall those specific seven minutes in the last three and a half days. "I...I think I did?"

I can relate to her confusion. If I'd messed up the process, I would have been hard-pressed to guess when.

The teacher sighs. "If you had, your potion would be mauve, like Lady Rhodes's, not green."

The beauty shoots me a furtive glare. I can't blame her. I would have preferred to be left out of the conversation. My peers scorn me enough as is.

"It's a good effort, truly, but a drop of that potion would send you straight to the grave in thirty seconds, tops. You'll get a B plus today."

I focus on the pan I'm washing, trying not to

grimace too obviously. I've only gotten As so far, in all disciplines, and I am doing my best to keep it that way.

Our teacher continues his inspection. Most students managed an acceptable potion, though he doesn't find another worthy of praise. One man, who produced a black bubbly brew, gets a failing grade.

Done with the cleaning, I return to my desk to put my affairs in order.

"Your Highness," Mr. Heffur says reverently, once again catching my attention.

Zale Devar is as gorgeous as usual, his pristine white shirt open at the throat spotless and wrinkle-free. The only thing even remotely out of place with him is his shoulder-length white-blond hair, but it's always artfully tousled in a purposeful style.

He's such a poser.

I don't have to check a mirror to know I look like hellhorses danced all over me. It's unfair that a man so powerful and influential also boasts the appearance of a young god.

I attempt to hide my curiosity, but I do listen in. I'd love to hear that His Highhandedness messed up today's work. Surely the universe would be so kind as to give me this tiny satisfaction?

"Another full mark!"

Dammit.

"If I may say so, it is a true pleasure to have two remarkable students in one class," our teacher gushes. "I've never had so many perfect scores in one term. There must be something in the Ravelyn water."

I can sense the gazes of the entire class focusing on

me, most of them resentful.

I should have a chat with Heffur, ask him to leave me out of such effusive praise in the future, if only to avoid getting stabbed in the back.

"Like that tramp's spawn ever tasted Ravelyn water," one short-haired, sophisticated brunette seethes.

She's taller than most, slender and dressed with care. I envy the sleek bob cut at her chin, if only because the style must take far less maintenance than my own stupid hair. Her sleeveless silver blouse, cut out under the breasts, would look downright lewd on most women, but her willowy silhouette allows it. Her leather skirt is short, but paired with thick, form-fitting pants and knee-high boots. If she didn't look like she'd love nothing more than to scratch my eyes out, I'd ask where she shops.

I'm taken aback by the level of spite in her voice.

It's not the first insult I've heard—not even the first this week—but it's delivered with disproportionate hostility. Maybe because her potion looks like something out of the wrong end of a dog—and smells like it, too.

The teacher clears his throat. "That was uncalled for, Lady Gyrth."

The name rings a bell, though I couldn't say where she's from, or anything else about her. Since the start of the year, my focus has been fixed on my schoolwork and nothing else.

I haven't tried to make friends. The school is filled with spoiled brats born with silver spoons in their mouths. How am I supposed to even communicate with the like of them? They dislike me because Zale Devar decreed they should.

"It's true," the woman insists, lips tight. "She's a common girl, born in the sewers of Magnapolis, no matter how many times you call her a lady."

Well, I suppose the duke did warn me that some might take umbrage to my heritage. Still, her tone's too resentful for someone I've never done anything to. I can't quite understand the extent of her animosity.

"Adelaid." That's all the king says, just her first name, but she immediately pinches her mouth shut, though she shoots me a deadly stare. "No need to engage the rabble."

She grins at the slight, expecting the words to wound me, I think.

They don't. I am part of the rabble, and I don't care. I won't have it any other way. Better a common girl with values and determination than a child riding on my family's fortune.

I feel no shame as to what I am. By the hells, I'm proud of it. Scientists say the brains of commons work slower, less efficiently than those of demis, and yet, in classes filled with their kind, I am the first.

Done organizing my bag, so as to avoid breaking any of the fragile utensils, I prepare to stand just as the king gets to his feet.

I immediately decide to plant my ass at my desk, to avoid moving in the same direction as him.

He drags his high-collared black jacket up his

shoulders and shoves his hands in his pocket before sauntering toward the door.

He doesn't bother to gather his stuff or clean up the mess on his work counter, arrogant bastard that he is.

I tense as his steps take him to the front of the room, but he walks past my desk this time, so I breathe out in relief.

Then, he stops.

"Come to think of it, Gyrth makes a fair point."

It takes me a while to realize he's talking to me while he's staring at the door, but he slowly turns and pins me with that unsettling and now familiar cold stare of his piercing blue eyes.

My heart starts to gallop in my chest. That can't be good. He doesn't interact with me directly, and I prefer it that way.

"You've yet to see your new country and pay your respects at court, Lady Rhodes." Irony drips from the two last words.

I've never hated a person before.

I despise the system designed to only serve the ruling minority, and I loathe the upper society as a whole for their utter contempt toward my kind, but individuals? I like or dislike someone depending on their behavior toward me. Hatred is extreme and personal. And yet I hate Zale Devar. I detest him because of his casual cruelty, because he thinks himself above me due to an accident of birth, and because he was given so many blessings and chose to become a toxic ass, rather than using them to help others.

We take three or four of the same courses and according to some of my teachers, my tests got the highest grades, so I am better than him—at studying, at least. Why can't he acknowledge that? Why can't he see we're all people with our strengths and weaknesses? He acts like I'm worth less than muck under his shoe because I am common and his ancestors trace back to an immortal who got locked away to another part of Xhera centuries ago. The very thought of him frustrates, unsettles, and irritates me like nothing else.

"You're summoned to court next weekend." His mouth curves into a smirk that shouldn't make him look more beautiful, given how cold it is. "Present yourself to your king on Baltaday."

"You're not my king," I grit between my teeth.

Even as the word escapes my lips, I know it's not entirely accurate. When I took my place as my stepfather's heir, I accepted a Ravelynian title. That means that I'm no longer a citizen of Magnapolis, or rather, not solely that.

I'm not sure I can decline an invitation from the king of Ravelyn, at least not without one hell of an excuse.

"Aren't I?" He huffs an amused laugh. "Then I suppose I shouldn't have the power to make you do anything I want."

Because he's mere feet away, I notice the subtle change in his pupils: his irises widen and the blue rims brighten so much it looks like a light was turned on inside him.

I can't look away. I can't even breathe.

"It would please me to see you leap onto your desk and remove all of your clothes, like the vulgar, inferior slut you are." His words might be crass, but his tone is hot chocolate wrapped in smooth velvet. Soft, low, sensual, and oh so beautiful.

My tongue darts out to lick my dry lips. I'm frozen in place, but if I could move, I'd obey him instantly. I want to please him. I crave his approval. It's only natural. He's the most beautiful man I've ever seen and I'd do anything to have him so much as smile at me.

At the back of my mind, something twitches, screaming for attention, but I barely hear it over the thundering need to satisfy his every whim.

You hate him. You hate him, you hate him, you hate him!

I don't. How could I?

I get to my feet, not even acknowledging the laughter around me, or our teacher's voice. I think he's talking to my beguiling, perfect king, and his tone is pleading, verging on panicked, but I cannot attend to a single word he's saying.

The strangest sensation washes over me, like a glass of cool water running down my back, distracting me from the lure of the beautiful siren before me. It's almost painful, but I instinctively cling to it as hard as I can, letting it anchor me to reality.

Straining, I lean over the desk toward the gorgeous thing trying to control me.

"No."

That's all I say, not trusting myself to remain another second in his presence.

I throw my satchel over my shoulder and leave the room, only breaking into a run after I'm out of view.

CHAPTER TWELVE
A BRUSH WITH DANGER

I run.

I run like my life depends on it.

I run away from everything in that room. Him, clearly, but also the side of myself I discovered while I was under his spell.

I've never been as elated and peaceful as I was for those few atrociously delectable moments. Shame and confusion mingle with the undeniable desire to feel that way again.

Even as I kick the door of my suite closed and lock it behind me, I fight the urge to return to the alchemy lab, get on my desk, and strip as my king demanded. Do anything he'd like at all, let him take control.

What in the seven hells was that?

I throw myself on top of my canopy bed, bite my pillow, and scream at the top of my lungs. My nails dig into my palms, and I welcome the pain. The reality.

And here I thought his ice was the most lethal power in his arsenal. Now I know better.

What he is?

It doesn't matter. Whatever the answer, I can't fight against it. Against him. I refuse to put myself back in the position of facing him, when I know I was so, so close to giving in.

Though alchemy is my favorite course, and the very reason I let Neleda convince me to come to this school, I have to drop out of the class and make sure I stay the hell away from him.

Except I can't. He summoned me to his court.

There has to be a way to avoid it. There must be.

I should fake a broken leg. All purgatories, I might as well really break my leg to escape it. His invitation has the stench of a trap all over it. I don't know what he has in store for me, but it can't be good.

I thought I hated him before, but it was nothing to the waves of rage now coursing through my blood. I'll never forgive how weak he just made me feel. Entirely out of control of the only thing that was ever truly mine, even when I had nothing else: my body. My soul.

I don't know how long I stay lying uselessly on my bed before I fall asleep. I worked for three days straight and before that, I don't think I stopped much. Not for six weeks.

Out of every thirty-hour day, I'm studying for at least twenty-five. I told myself I was eager to learn, but I'm starting to see the truth. What I am is hungry. I no longer have to worry about my safety or my next meal, courtesy of the man my mother married, but my character isn't going to change just because I get ten thousand golds every four weeks. I'll always be a lane kid eager for more.

My days used to be physically taxing, but it's my brain I've overused recently. I didn't recognize the signs of fatigue before. Now, I crash for an entire day, only awakening on Raverday afternoon with the biggest migraine I've ever had.

I grunt, dragging my heels to my bathroom, eyes half closed. I have to learn to be kinder to myself. Starting now. I take my time enjoying the shower. The hot jets feel pretty damn amazing. I can't believe I just rush in and out of there most of the time. I haven't even tried the bath tub.

"You and me, later, baby," I tell the lion-footed inanimate object.

My wardrobe is uninspiring as ever, but today, it grates on me. Not looking like myself sucks. I shuffle through hanger after hanger of clothing, attempting to find something that looks remotely like something Hel Stovrj might choose. All of my options very much belong to Helyn Stovrj-Rhodes. I end up picking a taupe blouse and a pair of green slacks, and I scowl at my reflection.

I need to go shopping.

I've only kept a hundred golds from my two first transfers. In the undercity, that would have bought me an entire new wardrobe, but up here, I'll be lucky if I can get a jacket for the contents of my bank balance.

I decide to go back to my neighborhood to shop, though there's no chance I'll blend if I wear downtown fashion.

Why does it matter? I didn't blend in wearing those idiotic, beige, boring-ass clothes either, courtesy of one Zale Devar, self-appointed royal pain in my ass. If I'm going to stand out either way, I might as well look like myself.

Reluctantly pulling my e-stone out of the bedside table, I check my test schedule. The moment I fire up the device, I wince, the screen hurting my eyes even more than usual. I never understood how other people could spend hours staring at screens. Within seconds, the brightness pains my eyes.

My next exams, History 201 and Psychology 302, aren't until next week, and I've already read the materials. I can take an evening off.

Before I question myself, I gather the pile of already-read library books on my desk and head out to return them. I can borrow the next ten I need, and get to work reading after I'm back from two essential trips.

I rush through the familiar halls as fast as I can. It's pretty late, and if I want to get to the day market before anyone respectable wraps up, I have to get going. I'd rather not deal with the Glitter Lane night market if I can help it.

I return my books borrow the next ones on my list, then I'm in my speeder, racing through the darkening streets of Magnapolis, a smile on my lips for the first time in weeks.

I'm going home.

CHAPTER THIRTEEN
A DANCE OF SNAKES

Nine weeks. In just nine stinking weeks, at the turn of the new year, I will reach my twenty-fifth winter and hold the reins of my kingdom.

Nine weeks until I have the authority to crush my enemies under my thumbs. The means to find out who they are in the first place.

I've requested to see the recordings of that fateful night so many years ago, and each time, I've received the same answer: the archives were tampered with, deleted without a trace. I've asked to see the days leading up to the massacre of my family, and was told nothing of consequence occurred. Whatever I try to uncover, my inquiry is brushed aside, ignored, redirected.

When I'm king, no one can stop me from finding out—even if I have to torture, threaten, and murder my way through the long list of witnesses.

Someone knows what happened. Someone saw

something. A guard, a servant—seven hells, I'll take a damn ghost if I must.

I have a simple plan in mind, and I'll implement it right after my coronation.

Then I'll have blood.

I've waited too long for this, and the upcoming end of my regency ought to be my only focus. Taking revenge for the death of my little sister should be the only thing on my mind.

And yet here I am, in a sunny floral drawing room decorated in silver and rose, drinking tea with the wife of one of the three people I suspect to be behind the massacre that almost cost me my life. That cost Moira hers.

Natheran Reiks once asked what it was like growing up without a parent, and I told him I've never known anything else. When my father was still alive, he was constantly occupied, either by affairs of state or with entertaining his extensive list of wives and courtesans. He paid attention to my brother, his heir, forming him for the crown he was supposed to eventually ascend to. I was his third-born, and too young to be of much use. As for my mother, she was but a pretty thing from his harem, and her primary concern was to keep her tits from sagging and her face from wrinkling. A half-coldblood from an insignificant line, born to an Anderkanian tradesman, she started to look like she was approaching her thirties at a hundred and seven years old. She knew what that meant: the moment she looked older than him, my father would have her replaced.

I was of little interest to either of my parents.

Reiks understood. His bastard of a father is worse than mine ever was, and has yet to do him the courtesy of dying.

I don't want revenge because someone killed parents I never cared about. I want revenge for Moira.

She was six. I remember the screams as the savages —stinking of sweat and the iron stench of common blood—ravaged her. They kept going after she died. I'll skin all of them alive before burning them, like they did her small, broken body.

Moira's memory is the one thing that has kept me alive for the last fifteen years. I learned to watch the shadows and turn blades. I poisoned myself until I was immune to whatever my enemies my might slip in my drinks. I slept only after plastering the walls of my chamber in three feet of ice each night. I have to live for her. It's that simple, and nothing else matters.

Instead I am having tea, because all of a sudden crushing an irrelevant, common mortal's spirit takes precedence over the full weight of my wrath.

I managed to ignore my curiosity and morbid fascination with the strange woman all season, but after what happened in alchemy, I can no longer afford to.

There's something going on with Helyn Stovrj. Something I'm missing.

I should have suspected it that very first night, when she, a common girl, held my interest. I barely understood myself, half disgusted, half piqued every time I saw her.

The nail in the coffin was her resisting my call,

although I pushed her. I pushed her harder than I've ever pushed anyone before. She should have been a pile of goo on the stone floor, begging me to let her serve me.

Instead, she refused me.

She could be in love. Those with true, deep connections are harder to crack. But I pushed so hard, she should have succumbed regardless. The barest hint of interest from me is enough for any man or woman to fall under my spell. Because she dared question me, I unleashed the entire brunt of my power on her, and still, she brushed it off.

Oh, she struggled. I could tell she was a heartbeat away from giving in. She still managed to deny it. Deny me.

I know powerful demigods incapable of such a feat. The freaking Frejr couldn't manage it, but she did.

I need to understand what she is. Which brings me to my tea companion: an annoying, overexcited, beaming woman with tight golden ringlets.

"Let me get this straight," I summarize the tale she shared at my request. "You popped out a kid and just left her to die the minute she was born."

Calm as ever, the blonde sips her tea before shaking her pretty head. "Well, no. I left her with my mother. Trust me, Your Highness, I know what I am, okay?" By this, she must mean a vicious snake. "But Lyn Stovrj was a good mother. She did her best for me. More than her best. I knew my girl would be a lot safer with her than she would ever be with me. And I was right."

I'm speechless. I momentarily consider freezing this

woman's heart in her chest, but I doubt that would work on someone this cold to begin with.

"I see how you look at me. But I was fifteen—a kid myself. I'd been raped by a guard who was not about to pay a dime to help raise his bastard. I didn't even know I was pregnant until the contractions started. I did what I thought was right at the time. Looking back, I'd make the exact same choice. I wasn't equipped to raise a child."

She has that much right.

"I can't tell you much about Helyn. I don't know her that well. I had to bribe half of the lane for what little knowledge I have, and it's secondhand. My own mother was tight-lipped. What I can tell you is that she's a lot better than I ever was." She grins over the rim of her teacup. "But you know as much, don't you? You wouldn't be here otherwise."

I lift my chin, staring at the poor excuse for a common mortal—and my view of common mortals wasn't exactly sterling to begin with.

"I saw your look in the garden that night. The longing. I get it. We almost have the same face, and boy, men were interested when I was her age." She chuckles. "And unlike me, she's also golden underneath the skin."

I have to reluctantly admire the duchess's candor. Still, we should get one thing straight. I return her honesty with a few truths of my own. "I don't long for your daughter, Neleda. I simply mistrust her, and you, and your husband."

The duchess takes one of her sickly sweet cupcakes and brings it to her pink lips. "I expect you do. Mistrust is a valid reason to stay away, right? And you want to stay away." She snorts. "My husband tells me you're quite the bigot. You only respect demis, and think coldbloods are better than anyone else. That's why he's so restrictive to you, you know. He realizes his power only extends for a few more weeks, and he dreads what you're going to do to his kingdom when you get to follow your whims. We bought land in other realms, just in case you drag us down with you."

I try to remember the last time I let anyone insult me like that, and I come up blank.

The nerve of the woman. "You're nothing but a fly, and you dare run your mouth at me?"

"Don't you know? I'm a duchess." She tilts her head. "Do you speak like this to other women of my rank?"

I want to tell her other duchesses don't earn their titles on their back, but I don't, because that wouldn't be true. In most couples, one of the pair marries up, either thanks to their riches or their beauty.

"The fact that I can't wield magik is all you can see. Your bias could cost you your crown, you know. For every demi, you have a hundred if not a thousand common subjects. Greater kings than you were toppled by those they saw as lesser."

My pulse races, and I grasp the arms of my chair to hold myself back. How dare she? She's nothing. She's...

Common.

She's common, and that's why I think she's nothing. I can't come up with another reason. Which means that she's right.

Sure, she's a terrible excuse for a parent, but so was my father. He barely spoke to me once a year, and sent servants to beat me when he decided I deserved a reminder of where I stood in the hierarchy of our family: at the bottom. And she does use her beauty as an advantage, but who doesn't in my court? Even I can be accused of such manipulation.

The entire reason for my disdain of this woman is the fact that she is common, and therefore, inferior.

Her pointing it out bothers me, although I know I've always held such beliefs. They just feel flimsy, when she brings them to light.

Maybe because her common daughter bore the full weight of my power and shrugged it off a day ago. I can't wrap my head around it. They are supposed to be weak.

How would you know?

I've never associated with any common for long enough to form an opinion of them. For a time, I just went with what I was taught to believe. Then, I truly started to hate them because I know the soldiers who hurt Moira had common blood. Even as a child, I could sense the difference between them and one of us.

I generalized, and the scholar in me dislikes the lack of proof and research to come to a conclusive opinion.

"I see more than your filthy blood, Duchess. I see you're smart enough to beat the odds, but have no moral compass. You have many skeletons in your closet, and you don't care. I see that you took one look at me in the garden and decided I'd be a wonderful prize to add to your achievements. You want me for your daughter because you think that reflects on you. You're a megalomaniac, and I don't doubt that if I had you investigated, I'd find you guilty of countless crimes." I pause and watch her stare at me with a steady, unbothered look that tells me everything I said was on the money. "I also see you thought you were doing the right thing, getting rid of the girl," I allow, to return her honesty. "And you might have."

"I did," she replies evenly, pouring herself another cup of tea. "You're sure you don't want a cupcake? They're delicious."

"I don't eat sweets." I never understood the mainlanders' fascination with confections.

"Your loss." She takes another bite, and moans in delight.

I grimace uncomfortably. She looks far too similar to Helyn, and barely older.

I hate that her appearance affects me more than I care to admit.

"Anything you can give me, Neleda." I stand. "You're an ambitious and ruthless soul. Surely you understand the value of a king owing you a favor."

I fully expect her to take the offer.

In a way, I'm not entirely wrong.

"She's proud, my daughter." Neleda smiles. "Proud of who she is, though it doesn't mean much to you. And that's why nothing you can do to her—nothing I ever did—will break her."

CHAPTER FOURTEEN

MEMORY LANE

T here's no one in the den. I don't find a single person on the rooftops of my old neighborhood, my crew's territory.

I parked the speeder at the edge of the undercity, uptown side, across the canal, and took my usual path through my town, if only because I miss it. And I didn't see the shadow of a soul.

The surfaces, usually spotless, courtesy of Khel, are covered by a sheen of dust. Either the crew had to move, or worse, they could have been arrested.

They could be dead.

Unsettled, I decide to get to the next point on my list of places to visit, in search of information as well as my initial quest.

It's almost dark by the time I get to the Glitter Lane, so I expect the market to be empty, but the artisans I planned to visit are still there.

Having a stand on the Glitter Lane is common for

most craftsmen of the undercity, whether they have a proper store or not. Once a royal way to travel from Flaur to the city, Glauter's Way is the widest street south of the river. It was unofficially renamed Glitter Lane a couple of centuries back, after one of the gaudy, extra Flaurian queens saw fit to have her servants throw glitter in front of her carriage as she travelled to town, or so the legend goes. Whether historically accurate or not, the name stuck and we've taken to throwing glitter and lighting fireworks at Yule.

The crews holding the territory changed hands a number of times over the years, because the location's the most prized in the undercity, though there's an understanding any crew can deliver goods to the Glitter Lane market. Unease still knots my insides. In my absence, there could have been a street war, or worse.

It kills me that I don't know for sure.

It's late enough in the day that some regulars closed shop, and a few of the evening stands are already set up. Drugs, gambling, dodgy enhancement offers. I've always kept my nose clean and well away from the night market.

"Well, I'll be damned." Hammon Kretcher eyes me from the tips of my toes to the swell of my chest under my blouse, never bothering to get to the eyes. Taking in my ridiculous outfit, he snorts. "If it isn't our Hel, all dolled up."

I wrinkle my nose in distaste, both at his leer and my clothing. I expected both, but dealing with him is unavoidable for two reasons: he's the biggest gossip I know, and he sells what I need. "Kretcher. Have you seen any of my crew around?"

"Yours, is it, still?" He chuckles. "If so, why don't you know where they are?"

I hide my irritation, knowing he thrives on annoying people as much as he can. "Why, indeed." I retrieve a fat red pouch filled to the brim and weigh it in my hand. "You think ten gold could jog your memory?"

His eyes widen. "Now you're talking my language. Word on the street is, they're spending time up at the orphanage—helping rebuild after the last fire, you know. That boy of yours is teaching some brats to read, too."

I grin and tilt my chin to his hand. "Say, you still have some of that armored fabric I got from you last year?"

He breaks into a grin and strokes his chin, always eager to get some business. "Hm. Why would you need it? If what I hear is true, and it usually is, no reason for anyone to shoot spells, bullets, and lasers at you anymore."

I shoot him my best fake smile. "I liked the look. Come on, Kretch. Everyone knows you can get anything."

Flattery rarely fails with simple men. "I don't have much left. You bought the last of the black. I have green, red, purple..."

He drags a box concealed underneath the loaded table to the side and retrieves several bolts of material.

That's more like it.

I spent what used to be a fortune on the familiar, featherlight fabric. Cool in the summer and spelled to retain body heat in the winter, the soft, silk-like weave can be used to make practically anything.

I still have my pants and cloak, but they were more useful than presentable.

"How much?"

His eyes take in the silk and linen I'm wearing. "Thirty per bolt. I don't have much left, see. It's popular. The pricing went up."

A bolt is enough for a cloak and three pairs of pants. He sold one to me at ten golds last year, and that was expensive for me. Now, I only bother to haggle out of habit—and because I know that whatever money I give him, he'll spend at one of the gambling parlors on the harbor. "Fifteen."

"No way. I can sell it to the Serpent crew across the river for twenty any day of the week."

Yeah, right. The Serpent crew is even more broke than my Claws.

Back in the day, the threat of giving away resources to the Serpents would have hit its mark. I hated those bastards. They always tried to get to the same jobs as I did.

I suddenly feel nostalgic and confused that I no longer feel any strong way about other crews. I just wish them well in their battle to survive this stinking city.

"They're getting their supplies from Jagger, not you. I can do seventeen. It's a lot more than what I spent last year, and you know it."

"Hey, I have mouths to feed! Twenty-five," he counters.

I snort again. "Your wife ran off with the baker and both your kids are of age."

"That doesn't mean they aren't still trying to suck me dry."

That, I can believe. "Twenty. That's my last offer."

He grumbles in agreement. "Which color, then?"

I look at the rich, forest green, not unlike the royal colors of Ravelyn. The second wouldn't usually be my style—I tend to avoid red, given how it clashes with my copper hair—but this crimson is so deep it looks almost black. I'm surprised I like it. The last is a bright, unapologetically regal purple. "I'll take all three."

Poor Kretch almost chokes on his gasp.

I've had my fun, so I take the bolts and make my way up the lane, until I reach the woman who's made my clothes for as long as I can remember.

The short, buxom tailor greets me with an unexpected hug, practically squeezing the breath out of me. "What you've done for the lanes," the old woman whispers against my cheek. "Oh, girl. Your grandma would be so freaking proud."

I'm all astonishment. Alva wasn't supposed to let anyone know I was sending money. If there's one thing the undercity folk like less than fancy nobles from uptown, it's a handout from one of them. "Err, Johel?"

"Yes, yes. Not a word, I know. But my boy keeps nothing from me."

I'd forgotten: Khel. His parents died when he was

young, and was taken care of by his aunt, Johel. They look nothing alike, so the familial relationship was easy to overlook.

"Tell me. What do you need, hm? Fancy-schmancy court clothes, yes?"

I came for the exact opposite, but now that she mentions it... "I guess?" The reminder that I'm supposed to turn up to the Ravelyn court this weekend grates. I'll do my damnedest to escape that summons, but I doubt I can avoid the court forever. It'll help to have something to wear. "But I came looking for everyday stuff, you know." I'm tired of skirts, and those stupid slacks should be burned. "Just a little less practical than what I used to wear, but nothing fancy. I guess I'd like a dress, maybe a skirt, three pairs of pants, and a dozen tops." That should be more than enough. I never owned that much clothing at one time when I lived in the lane. "I got the same fabric as last year from Kretcher down the lane. You can use it for some of that, and I'll pay for linen and cotton otherwise. Just start an account."

"Everyday stuff," she mumbles. "You're Hel Stovrj, not an everyday girl." Her expert gaze takes me in. "I see you haven't changed much. Leave the bolts with me. I'll make the first delivery by the end of the week, yes?"

I hesitate. She's dressed me for as long as I can remember. Grandma Lyn paid her in salves and remedies when I was a kid and after I took to the lanes, I paid her myself, either in trade or in gold, when I could afford it. I decide to trust her. "I'll make a deposit for the fabric you need."

"A deposit?" She laughs so hard she bends down and holds her thick thighs. "You'll give me nothing, dear girl. You've fed half the kids around here and sent the rest to school."

"That's kind of you, but I can afford it, and you have to keep a roof over your head." I take her hand in one of mine, retrieve my coin pouch, and place it in her grasp.

I only brought a hundred and fifty golds with me. She can have what's left of it.

"No. Your money's no good here."

"Of course it is." I step back and hold both hands up, refusing to touch the pouch she holds out to me. "If you want to give it away, that's your business. It's yours to squander."

"Now listen, young lady!" Johel glares, and holds one finger up. She scowls, holding my steady gaze, before remembering that I'm stubborn as all purgatories. With a grunt of resignation, she says, "You're going to get the best dress ever seen in the history of their dumb frozen court, you hear?"

That's frightening. "Well, where I live now, people are a little understated. Classy, you know." I think back to Adelaid Gyrth's bare midriff, and compress my lips. Classy isn't the best description, but the nobles certainly don't dress in the lanes' idea of high fashion. "I'm not after a meringue."

Swift as the wind, she swats my back with my bolt of fabric. "Get out of here before I turn your hide red. Meringue, my wrinkled ass. The nerves on you!"

I chuckle, and opt to retreat. If she makes me something dreadful, I'll just give it away.

It doesn't really matter. When I finally have to go to Ravelyn, I'll be ridiculous either way.

Zale Devar will make sure of it.

Time to attempt to weasel out of my summons.

CHAPTER FIFTEEN

THE RULES OF THE GAME

I am astonished to find my speeder where I left it, and unbesmirched to boot.

Parking a vehicle of that price range just across the canal from my old neighborhood is nothing short of inviting mischief. Hel of the Claws would have keyed the matte paint for sheer spite. I consider stopping by the orphanage to catch up with Alva, but it's getting dark; I don't have time to get roped into helping out with construction work. I can come back to the crew later.

On ride back uptown, my fingers dancing on the control panel, I realize that most of my anxiety is gone. I should have returned to my neighborhood much sooner. I'm a fish out of water at Five, and occasionally, I should plunge back into my tank to breathe.

I even feel better about my altercation with Zale. Sure, he's one hell of a dangerous freak, but I was aware of that before yesterday. I'll just have to stay clear of him as much as possible, starting with getting out of his summons.

I lower the speeder to ground level when I get to Stateside, and glide up to the gate of the Rhodes residence. I only have time to open my window half an inch before the automated barrier unlatches. Whoever's guarding the gate must have had a description of my speeder. The model's certainly not hard to identify.

Objectively, the vehicle is beautiful, and if someone had asked me what kind of transport I'd love to own when I was twelve, I might have dreamed up something quite like it: a cotton candy blue convertible built for racing, sun powered, with wide bumpers and silver accents. It's no less ridiculous. I would have returned it, but to travel all the way from Five to the lanes on foot would take me over an hour each way. Asking for another choice of speeder would have felt too much like being the spoiled daughter, and I'm not about to take that position. I keep my communications with the duchess to a bare minimum.

Yet here I am, entering her home.

I leave the speeder in front of the main entrance to the red brick house. A footman dressed like a penguin swings the dark green double doors, bowing low as I pass him by. "Lady Rhodes."

By now, I'm almost used to that strange new name of mine.

Stovrj is a common northern name. Grandma Lyn told me her husband's folk used to come from Vanemir. She herself was a daughter of Flaur, though she left for

Magnapolis in search of work when she was younger than me. Her maiden name was Beauchamp, a farmer's line of no note.

The Rhodes have been around for so long I can name some of them from history books referring to events from before the common era, in the days immortals roamed Xhera as they pleased. The family isn't truly local to Ravelyn—they have a foothold in practically every kingdom, except maybe Dorath. Every single one of them is either rich, a noble, or both. And now I'm one of them, according to the new edition of the peerage for sale. I bought a copy after the duke showed me his, just to check.

I learned to drive and pilot at nine, with one of Grandma Lyn's gentleman friends—the butcher on Goblesquare. He had a small hovercart to deliver his meats to the restaurants all over the undercity, and he showed me how to operate it so that I could make a buck helping him out occasionally. I never bothered to file for a permit; no one checks licenses in the lanes, and I didn't go anywhere else. One of the formalities I had to complete was passing driving and flying tests this summer. The permit that arrived in the post was my first glimpse at this strange new life. Next to my photograph, the holographic card read "Lady Helyn Stovrj-Rhodes, 7 Green Lane, Stateside, Magnapolis." I stared at it for a full ten minutes, and when I passed it around, Alva did the same.

"Ms. Helyn." A tall, pale servant with a face so skeletal I half expect him to keel over in the next breath comes down the grand staircase leading to the two upper levels.

I can't for the life of me recall his name, but I know he's the duke's butler.

"I don't believe you are expected." I note his odium in the arch of his eyebrow as well as his judgmental tone.

Luckily for me, I couldn't care less.

"I didn't call ahead."

"Well, it is your home." His lips press even thinner, and I smirk, highly amused.

He clearly disapproves of me, but a professional such as he isn't about to make it more obvious than a subtle change of expression. "I'm afraid your lady mother is away at this time. Shall I arrange for refreshments while you wait?"

Perfect! "That's all right. I'm here to see the duke, if he's at home and can spare a moment."

Both surprise and suspicion flash in his beady eyes. "I'll inform His Grace of your arrival. Would you care to sit in the library, the drawing room, or shall I open up your bedroom?"

Though he hasn't said it in so many words, this jerk is implying I might wish to bed my ancient stepfather. I could vomit, but I hide that his barely veiled barb offends me.

"I can wait right here, pal." As I hoped, my familiarity makes his weak chin twitch.

I lean against the marble wall.

"I believe the duke would prefer if you made yourself comfortable."

In other words, he might get an earful if he's seen treating me as less than an honored guest.

Good.

"I'm perfectly comfortable here. I'd be more so if you could get my mother's husband, so I can be on my way."

The pale butler's eyes flash. I can practically feel energy crackle around me. If we were in a dark alley, I'd be in trouble with this demi, but we're in Salvar Rhodes's home, and he's but a servant. Cutting his scowl short, he returns to the second floor, muttering unintelligible curses under his breath.

I can't afford to make another enemy, even a servant, but whatever I do, this one isn't about to be my friend, so I don't mind infuriating him.

Never one to waste time if I can help it, I look through my bag, and pick up the e-stone I rarely use. I ignore the instant pressure at the back of my skull and check the university platform for any updates.

There's a metamorphosis lab I could attend in two days, covering how to change a rock into a living thing. As the requirements are an intermediate understanding of shifter biology, but no specific magik skills, I could take it. The attendance would count toward my science credits, but it clashes with an astronomy class.

If given a choice, I'd much rather study the stars than stare at a rock for hours on end, but I haven't done much metamorphosis. I'm weighing the benefit of each option, half wishing I could turn back time and attend both, when the duke's booming voice resounds through the vast entry hall. "Helyn!"

Affable as ever, my stepfather makes his way downstairs from the second floor, ahead of his grim butler.

He's dressed in a formal red and gold velvet cloak, though the city is still hot at the end of the summer. "What a surprise. I do hope you'll stay for dinner."

Not on my life. "I have to get back to the library. Too many tests coming up." It's a weak excuse, but he doesn't expect a different answer.

"Well, what can I do for you?"

Save my skin.

I do stick to the truth, though I don't bother to spell out the nitty gritty. "The king has summoned me to court. I'd much rather not travel that far this weekend." Or ever. "You know. Tests."

I need to write down a list of better excuses, but in the meantime, that's all I have.

His eyes widen. "The king himself?"

I shrug both shoulders, to convey some of my indifference and a degree of confusion.

"Helyn, Helyn... Well, I'm aware you're not familiar with court protocol, so let's play this out. I could write to inform him that you're otherwise engaged—"

"Great!" I say before he can add another word. There's definitely a "but" coming, and I'd rather not hear it. "So, that's sorted."

"Hardly." Reaching the bottom of the stairs, the duke shakes his head. "As I said, I could, but it's not an advisable course of action. For you or me."

I want to scream. "This weekend is really not a good time."

He's undeterred. "If the herald of the crown had extended an invitation and you had declined, you'd have to give a very compelling reason, as well as a thousand apologies, excuses, and plenty of gold to make sure he's not offended." The duke gestures to an open door, and I follow him.

Inside, the dark wood and red leather creates an atmosphere that is surprisingly homey. He moves to a large bar and pours two glasses of a dark amber liquid.

I accept the one he offers, though I'm not too fond of liquor. By the sound of it, I'm going to need it.

"The herald would be offended regardless. Which means more taxes, more appearances required during the dullest of events for at least a decade."

I'm not certain my increasingly acute headache is solely due to my use of the e-stone.

"And you were invited by the king, not a pompous glorified secretary. Should you decline, not only will the herald take it as a deadly affront—condemning you to a lifetime of tedious attendance—but the rest of the court will also give you the cold shoulder. Even if you had compelling reasons. There's nothing you are not expected to reschedule to accommodate the king's courtesy."

His courtesy. That's rich.

I guess I'm right back to breaking my own bones to justify my absence. Though by the sound of it, Salvar Rhodes would simply push me around in a wheelchair.

I down the drink in one go and my throat burns in protest. "Ew."

"That was a two-thousand-mark usquebaugh. You're supposed to savor it."

"Savor what?" I grimace as he chuckles.

"You should come back for a drink more often, refine your palate. I'll make a connoisseur out of you."

He's warm as ever, and I'm still entirely uncomfortable because I have no idea what he wants. There must be more to this story than him needing an heir and randomly accepting a street urchin.

I won't find out today, and the longer I stay here, the more risk I take of running into Neleda. Time for a strategic retreat. "I'd better get back to my books."

The duke nods and accompanies me back to the entry hall. "Your mother will be sorry to have missed you."

Perhaps she might, but missing her is the first stroke of luck I've had in a while.

"Helyn?" the duke calls just as I reach the front doors, already open by one of the footmen.

I look over my shoulder.

"This Baltaday is Lughnasadh."

I nod. "Yeah, I know."

"And the king asked for you, specifically," he hedges, his tone making it clear he expects me to understand something, beyond the wheel of the year calendar.

I can't see what he means, so I do turn to face him. "So?"

The duke stares at me for a while, but ends up

simply shaking his head. "It's not my place to speculate His Grace's desires, but you may wish to prepare yourself."

A shiver travels down my back. "For what?"

"Anything."

CHAPTER SIXTEEN

HALF THE BATTLE

T he duke's ominous last words stay with me all
week, running around in circles in my brain.

"That's an unusual request, Lady
Rhodes." The advisor adjusts his monocle to check my
file. "You only need two hundred credits and one lab to
complete that course."

I wipe my sweaty palm over my beige skirt. "My
schedule's too taxing. I need to drop something," I lie.

Or maybe I'm just sharing a partial truth. I have
bitten off a ton this term.

"Well, in that case, might I suggest arithmetic?
You've completed your mathematic requirements
already, and the subject doesn't quite align with the rest
of your courses."

I purse my lips. "I'd like to shelve alchemy until next
term, please."

The old man stares straight at me over the rim of
his one lens. I don't know what he sees, but after one
long, disappointed sigh, he nods once. "Very well. I'll

give you a week to come to your senses. If you don't, I'll see that you're moved out of the course. Do keep in mind it is possible that Professor Heffur might refuse to teach you a second time, however. It's his prerogative to decline working with students he believes might waste his time."

I swallow hard. It's my favorite discipline; if I can come out of Five with one title, I'd like it to be alchemist. Can I take that risk?

Can I not?

"One week, Lady Rhodes."

I take his last words as an invitation to go, thank him, and retreat.

Despite my stepfather's warning, I try to get out of Zale's summons.

The duke warned me I might suffer the court and the king's wrath for declining. What he didn't understand is that I already am on Zale's shit list. He sets the tone wherever he goes, so my shunning is guaranteed whatever I do.

On Luprday, I get a decorous formal invitation, calligraphed in complex cursive. I answer the return address—right here in Magnapolis, on Royal Lane—to inform the sender I can't attend court.

Fifteen minutes later, I get another letter on thick parchment. The note reads "Your king has summoned you. Fail to attend and face the consequences."

There's no signature, no address, but I can just tell the rushed, elegant scrawl is from him.

I dread to think what the consequences he'd design for me might be—presumably something worse than whatever he's planned this weekend.

I'm screwed either way. The only question is how hard.

Instead of studying for my next tests, as I'm fairly well prepared and incapable of concentrating today, I dig out obscure, seldom-read volumes on the customs of Ravelyn in the library.

I hoped a degree of understanding about that elusive northern court might help, but instead of feeling better, my anxiety increases with each line of the dusty books.

I'm appalled by the barbaric customs of the two islands.

A country mostly populated by bears, seals, and wolves, Ravelyn was originally two prisons, built in the north and south poles. Gods and mortals sent offenders they didn't want to or couldn't kill, either to be banished or locked away.

The commons died in time, but immortals are hard to kill, and their descendants adapted to the extreme temperature, becoming the demi subrace we now call coldbloods.

They aren't just one type of demi, like witches or shifters or the fair folk; coldbloods may be any of the above, and hold power over the temperature on top of it.

That explains how Zale Devar almost managed to

steal away my will. His primary power is manipulating minds, not ice.

The more I read about the line of the monarch ruling over the frozen wasteland, the more certain I am that I never should allow myself to stand within ten yards of the evil bastard.

After the gods were sent to the eternal realms, the prisons at the poles were demolished, and one halfblood earned the title of king in the north by tearing everyone who objected apart: Tryn Du Var, a bloodsucking monster banished from Flaur.

The Du Var line issued from a mortal and Velenor himself. As in the god of the shade, personification of evil on Xhera.

Witches and demis have long waged a campaign to explain that shade and light are simply elemental magiks, and that using one or the other doesn't define anyone's character. I call bullshit. There's a reason why children are afraid of the dark, why the horrors happen in the shadow. Dark witches have been known to manipulate corpses. I don't care if they like bunnies and butterflies. If Velenor and Mara, goddess of light, appeared in front of me, I know which one I'd be running away from, screaming at the top of my lungs: the king of shade.

Tryn reinvented himself as Devar, rejecting the family that banished him, and became the first king of northern Ravelyn. Then he set out to take the southern pole and dethroned the queen of crows who ruled there. He must have either seduced or raped her, because she bore his heir. She was high fae, and their child inherited both of their power, as well as all of their wickedness.

The Devars aren't bloodsuckers or fair folk, they're the worst of both.

I stop reading and shut the book, frustrated and sufficiently terrified.

Grandma Lyn was of the mind that knowledge is power, and she transmitted that belief to me. Now I have concrete proof she was right. If I'd known everything about Zale Devar earlier this summer, I would have learned to curtsy and keep my mouth shut, except to say "yes, sir."

I snort, recognizing my self-deception. I know better. Even aware of the consequences, I wouldn't have been able to make myself small to placate him. It's not in my nature.

I return to my suite and start the ritual I am fast getting used to at the end of the day: preparing a bubble bath, with flutes and piano playing in the background.

I've only just sunk into the delightfully warm water when a knock at my door disrupts my enjoyment.

I groan, pout, but get out of the tub all the same. "Coming!"

Two dorm employees greet me, armed with several boxes each. "Delivery for one Helyn Stovrj?"

I'm confused and chary, but my expression clears when I realize Johel did say she'd send clothes this week.

I open my door wide to let them in, just as Zale walks past my room, dressed all in black, hands in his pockets, and followed by half a dozen students, all as pale and slender as he.

I recognize Gyrth from alchemy, but the rest are unfamiliar.

I tense, expecting a confrontation, but if the king sees me, he doesn't acknowledge me.

Shit.

He knows where my suite is now. I shut my door, and lock it for good measure.

"Where do you want the packages, my lady?"

Oh.

I completely forgot about the delivery.

"My bed, if you please." I lead the way, out of the hall and into the beige, tragically boring, luxurious, and immense room.

It took me days to get used to the sheer size of the place. I keep the curtain closed most of the time, just to retain some semblance of the sense of encasement I'm familiar to.

I give a gold to each woman and accompany them out before locking myself in again.

Curiosity wins over my desire to return to my bath, so I open my delivery.

My jaw drops when I unwrap package after package. I trust Johel to manage simple, practical clothing, as I've worn her work most of my life. I never knew she could sew complex layers, shaping skirts like a floral blossom, or a mermaid's tail, or stitch golden thorns and roses, moon crescents and delicate birds along hems.

At least I'll go to the pillory in style.

CHAPTER SEVENTEEN

FOOL'S DAY

T'm not myself on Lughnasadh. The high level of magik in the air, along with the weakness my line has for all form of excess, means that I'm likely to be drunk on nothing until morning.

Tonight is the one night I'm nothing more than what my blood makes me: a shade, feeding on the most sinful of indulgences.

And I've already chosen my prey.

Helyn's conspicuous absence in the alchemy lab that started yesterday afternoon amuses and irritates me.

Like any predator, it entertains me to see my little mouse attempt to run, but I expected to see her, taunt her today. Without her furtive glances, her straight spine, and the way she jumps every time she hears my name, the lab is utterly dull.

I chose alchemy because I understand most aspects of magiks, and needed to expand my knowledge in one of the few branches that remained obscure to me, but after seven weeks, I can summarize this practice in one single word: tedious.

Watching Helyn squirm is my only source of entertainment, especially on days like today.

I should have known she'd miss this class. She's supposed to be at my court tonight; she's likely already on her way. Unless she dared defy me. I grin, savoring both prospects. I'd rather have her tonight, during a festival when I, and the rest of my court, let the monsters out, but either way, she'll be at my mercy.

I finish enchanting the stone—to remain warm for a year—hours ahead of the other students, and in the back of my mind, I wonder how long it would have taken Helyn to get the job done. Would she have beaten me again?

Heffur invites me to leave early, and I make my way down the tower of magiks, eager to get going.

My stomach grumbles when I pass the dining hall, and I hesitate. There will be plenty to consume at court, but it is Lughnasadh. I'm starving, and in more way than one.

Spotting a familiar figure by one of the fireplaces, I decide to play a game before the festivities. "Frejr."

The slender brunette my oldest friend decided to claim long ago directs her large green eyes at me, mouth parted.

Natheran Reiks was an imposition I rejected the moment it was thrust on me. The very thought of getting close to the future king of one of the mainland realms seemed ludicrous, but my regents arranged for him to spend the summer at Whyte Fort. I fully intended to ignore him. He had other ideas. We've been communicating ever since, albeit privately. I don't want my enemies to be aware of my alliances.

Two years ago, he wrote me a simple, direct note completely out of character: *Alis Frejr is off-limits.* I didn't need more to understand his intentions.

I can see the reasons behind Reiks's fascination with the witch, though she's hardly my type. I would never choose a partner who's likely stronger than me. There's only enough room for one massive ego in my bed.

"Devar," she counters. "You're in this dorm?"

I consider my answer. I have a suite reserved for me here, and in the common dorm, though I rarely use either bed, for anything other than a roll with a student in the middle of the day. When in town, I prefer to use the Devar house on Royal Lane.

I could tell her as much, but there's a reason why I have several options. I'd rather no one knows where I sleep. "Why wouldn't I be?"

"I never noticed you."

If this had come from anyone else, I might have been wounded, but Alis Frejr stays away from the crowd. She isn't pushed to the sidelines like Helyn—she avoids everyone, either out of fear or contempt, I can't quite decide. "I suppose not. That would have required lifting your eyes from your tiptoes occasionally."

I can tell I've upset her, as her green eyes flash with enough magik to make a lesser man wet his pants.

Reiks is an idiot, tangling with this thing.

"Are you coming to the Lunar Club tonight?"

Her question surprises me.

I didn't expect her to show any form of interest toward me. In the years she's spent here, she's kept a purposeful wall between herself and the rest of Five, yet, her enquiry sounds almost like an invitation. "Why?" I sit on a chair close to hers, fascinated by this strange woman my friend took a liking to.

Really, we ought to get to know each other. She'll marry Reiks, and I'll stand as his witness before the year is out, if he has his way.

And the heir to Anderkanian crown generally does.

"Why would you come?" She seems confused. "I don't know. I assumed you were invited."

I chuckle. "I meant, why do you care if I'm showing up?" It's just not like her.

She attended one of the meetings Reiks likes to hold with the rest of the future—and current, in my case—leaders attending Five, and she did her best to blend in with the furniture.

Now she's engaging me.

In the last five weeks or so, something fundamental about her has changed. If it weren't Lughnasadh, I might care to find out what.

She purses her lips. "I was making conversation."

"Mmkay." I lie back, increasingly amused. "So long as that's all. I don't poach pretty faces from my friends, tempting though they can be."

I'm flirting a little, because I can't stop myself this time of the year, but I'd seriously never attempt to seduce her in earnest. Mostly because Reiks would kill me in my sleep if I was serious. He's never been possessive of women before, and we've shared a fair number of conquests in the past, but Alis Frejr is it. His future queen. Once he makes his mind up, there's no changing it, and he's had his eyes on her for much longer than she knows.

"I—I wasn't..." She looks horrified, poor thing. "I'm not—"

"Interested? You're gay, I take it." She isn't, but I can't help teasing her.

I'm in the mood for mirth and games, enthused by what I have in store for a certain hapless vixen later.

"I'm not gay," she grumbles.

"Ah. In love, then." Reiks will be glad to hear it.

She half laughs, half chokes. "Absolutely fucking not."

"The lady doth protest too much." I lean forward and whisper, "Let me tell you a secret, Frejr. No one can resist me. I need sex to survive, so my kind has evolved to appeal to every other creature. Even goddesses would fall at my feet if I wished them to. There are few exceptions on Xhera."

One such exemption comes to mind.

"The one exception is men and women in love—or not interested in my sex, naturally."

And Helyn Stovrj.

I dug into Helyn this week, and I doubt she's ever been in a relationship, let alone one deep enough to build shields against my power. Her resistance is, shockingly, innate.

No common girl ought to have such power over me, yet she does. No common girl should have been able to beat me in tests or do better than the rest of our class, either.

I have come to the conclusion Helyn is not entirely common—or my knowledge of their kind is a lot weaker than I care to admit.

"I'm not in love with anyone." She shakes her head for good measure. "Not even a little bit."

I smile at the poor Frejr girl indulgently. "You haven't completely fallen yet, that's true. I could fill you with desire if I set out to." I can sense I'm stirring her more than I did Helyn in alchemy, and I'm not even using much of my influence. And I won't. Early demise holds no appeal to me. "Don't fret. You're safe from me."

"Good. Keep me out of your power plays."

I'm amused she thinks I'm trying to enter a pissing contest with Reiks when I am, in fact, doing him a favor—and admittedly, entertaining myself.

"Sorry, sweetling. Just checking if I have lost my touch." I wink at her.

I'm not joking. Her weakness to my appeal was a balm to my soul after Helyn. "Apparently not."

She practically flies out of her chair, and I chuckle, retrieving my e-stone.

Moving to the buffet to grab a bunch of grapes, I shoot a raven to Reiks.

I lured your girl a little. She didn't fall over the floor in a puddle of lust.

Keep your dick well away if you want to retain it, Zale.

I chuckle on my way to my hovercraft.

CHAPTER EIGHTEEN
A TOUCH OF MAGIK

O ver the course of the week, I spend my time first attempting to avoid going to Ravelyn, and then, trying not to think about the fact that I can't decline the summons.

It's only when I wake up on Baltaday morning that I register that in my denial, I failed to arrange a transport to take me there in the first place.

The royal court is held in the north isle, almost two hundred thousand miles away. How am I supposed to be there at the twenty-fifth hour?

The only option at my disposal is taking my speeder, but I'm not comfortable enough as a pilot to travel halfway across the globe, flying over the Silent Sea. I may have started driving a long time ago, but I seldom got the chance, and never for long distances. Besides, I don't know the way. I could use a navigation hologram, but my reaction to tech would make it dangerous. The only thing worse than an inexperienced pilot behind the monitor is one with a pounding headache.

After spending most of the gold I had left on Glitter Lane, I doubt I have enough money to charter a hovercraft. The duke's allowance comes like clockwork, on Raverday every four weeks. I'll get the next injection of funds after this weekend.

I look into public transport and groan. By train, then boat, and finally, communal sled to reach the capital, Oslov, the journey would take almost the entire weekend.

There's no way around it. I have to ask for a favor from the last person I want to be indebted to.

I drive to my mother's red brick house for the second time this week, hoping to once again deal with her husband.

I've run out of luck.

Their reaper of a butler informs me that the duchess will receive me in her parlor. I suppose he doesn't want to risk my opting to remain in the hall this time.

No sooner have I sat on her floral cushioned sofa than Neleda enters the small, elaborate antechamber, radiant in a complex damask gown that changes color with the light, red one moment, black the next. "Helyn! I didn't think I'd see you before court."

"You're going to Ravelyn tonight?"

As she and her husband have been in town every time I stopped by the house, this week or before the start of the term at Five, I assumed they didn't spend a lot of time up north.

"Like I'd miss my own daughter's presentation."

Why not? She's missed everything else.

In no position to give her lip when I came to ask for help, I choose to keep my thoughts to myself, for once. "Would you mind if I accompany you? I don't want to take the speeder all the way there."

Eyes wide, she seems shocked and horrified, either by the notion of my piloting alone so far, or by my asking her for something. Both, in all likelihood.

"Yes, certainly you may. Sal is having luncheon at his club today, so we'll leave right after, in an hour or two." She eyes me from head to toe. "You're not wearing that, are you?"

I'm in one of Johel's new outfits: a green, corseted short tunic in my armored material, flaring at the hips and ending high on my thighs. I paired with one of the half-dozen form-fitting, comfortable black pants she sent me.

I love it, because I look like myself—at least, what the old Hel would have worn if she'd had enough money to burn on looking pretty. What I don't look like is a duke's heir.

Part of me wants to tell Neleda that I'll indeed wear exactly this to the court gathering I'd prefer not to attend, in hopes that the news might make her choke or expire on the spot of a heart attack, but I do need a ride.

Though presumably, if my mother died, I might be excused.

"I have a gown in the speeder. I planned on getting changed closer to the time."

My summons is over twelve hours away. Sweating

in my clothes all day hadn't seemed like the best course of action.

"Oh, very well. It just dawned on me, I hadn't had anything sent to you for tonight. I'm pleased you thought to order a gown." She sighs in visible relief.

I perversely wonder what she'd say if I let her know that said gown came from the lanes. She'd be horrified. Even I hadn't truly trusted Johel to deliver, right up until the moment I unpacked her work.

I might have been right not to, anyway. I have no idea what one wears to any court. All I know is that I love every single piece she sent, tonight's gown most of all.

I hesitated to bring it, lest my experience in Ravelyn ruins the garment for me, but I opted to all the same. At least I can walk in there with a degree of confidence, if only on the surface.

"We'll arrive too close to tonight's celebration to have time for more than a touchup when we get to the Whyte Fort. Why don't I have your gown sent up? My maid can dress you and see to you while we wait for the duke."

She doesn't trust me to know what to do with my face or my hair, and she's not wrong.

Neleda is always put together in a way I could never be, but today, she's a vision, her skin glowing and her hair braided in complex waves around her pretty face.

I nod, willing to take the aid of whichever maid is responsible for her transformation.

If I manage to look the part, the ordeal that tonight is likely to be might be a little less mortifying.

I tell myself that much, though I know Zale Devar will do whatever is in his power to ensure I don't come out of his realm unscathed.

I'm walking into a lion's den and I have no idea what to expect.

My mother leads us out of the parlor and into a bedroom that blends her style preference—exuberance and rich color—with the dark wood and leather look the duke favors.

I glance at the enormous bed, still unmade, and grimace in distaste.

We thankfully don't linger, moving on to a well-appointed dressing room, larger than my crew's underground den.

She rings a bell, and a coldblood woman soon appears. Shorter than most of her race, she distinguishes herself by having dark hair and a discreet layer of blush applied to her cheeks.

"Your Grace." She bows low to my mother, and if she thinks herself above serving a common, she hides it well.

"Triffa, this my daughter Helyn. You wouldn't mind working your magic on her, would you? She's to be presented at court tonight."

"How wonderful!" She beams at me, and rushes to my side. "And on Lughnasadh, too. Sit, sit!"

She leads me to a low, pink velvet stool in front of an ornate standing mirror taller than me.

"You've been before?" I ask. "To court."

"Oh, no, not me, my lady." Without further ceremony, Triffa undertakes the momentous task of untangling my hair, using her fingers, first. "I'm a maid."

I've seen the servants in this household, and they don't behave or dress like her.

Triffa's gown is made with a simpler material, but it's nigh on as well-cut as my mother's.

"Well, we'll remedy that, won't we, Triffa?" my mother offers. "You can come with us to Whyte Fort tonight, and attend us before we greet the king."

The maid gasps happily. "You're too good to me!"

"Nonsense." Neleda waves a dismissive hand. "I'll have a footman carry your gown if your speeder's unlocked?"

I don't remember whether it is, so I hand my mother the plastic key card, glad to watch her leave.

Once Triffa's satisfied most of my knots are gone, she switches to a brush. "What luxurious tresses, my lady. I know ladies who'd kill for such a vibrant color."

I understand why my mother favors her, then. This woman's kind tongue is all the encouragement anyone needs. It's not the words, so much as it is the fact that she seems to mean them.

"I don't mind the color. It's the curls I can't abide." I huff. "I don't have time to brush for hours every day."

"You don't need to." The servant shakes her head fervently. "I'll talk to your mother about sending up a lotion for you to use instead of soap. Now mind, you're to air dry your hair and tie it up before sleep, and apply the balm I'll make for you nightly, yes? Your curls won't need any brushing at all. Just run your fingers through them in the morning."

If she's telling the truth, her knowledge is worth her weight in gold. "Would it have any magik, that balm?"

She grins. "Only a smidgen. You don't mind, do you?"

I hesitate.

I don't have much against magik, but I don't trust it either, as it's often used against the interest of people like me.

That said, my hair's one problem that can't be fixed by mundane means. "I don't mind."

"Good, good. Now let's make you shine."

And she does just that.

CHAPTER NINETEEN

THE DANGERS OF THE NORTH

The duke's hovercraft is the largest vehicle I've ever seen, let alone travelled in.

It flies silently through the darkening clouds, so steady I might have believed it to be in a building, immobile and on the firm ground, if not for the mesmerizing view out of the window.

I've never travelled outside of Magnapolis, and all of a sudden, I see the thick, green forests of Vanemir, then the glistening river marking the border of Flaur, and the endless fields of golden crops and luxuriant plains.

Soon we're flying over the Silent Sea, seemingly calm from up high, though it owes its name to the number of ships that never come back to shore, sunk by its treacherous, unpredictable waters.

We've flown for under an hour when everything turns white.

I can't deny that Ravelyn is beautiful—an endless

horizon covered in snow. I squint, noticing smudges in the otherwise uniform view.

"Are those villages?" I wonder.

We're a good fifty thousand feet in the air, so it's hard to tell.

The duke rises from his armchair to join me at the window I've barely left since we took off.

I'm too nervous to sit.

"Mayhaps. We're over the Silver Woods, not far from Ostrov. There are a few settlements around here. It's hard to tell from above this time of the year—the snow covers the rooftops."

We're in the summer! "Is there any time of the year when the snow doesn't?"

He chuckles. "We clean the snow off on Beltane. You'd be surprised at the change of scenery: the tiles are bright reds and blues and greens."

I'm too surprised to comment one way or another. Ravelyn's always been a bland, frozen realm in my mind, and I can't reconcile my idea of it with the fact that its inhabitants like cheerful tiles, just like the houses in the lanes.

"We're almost there. See those mountains right ahead?"

I have to focus, but in time I do distinguish the shape of five high mounts, set up in a circle.

"The castle is on one of those peaks?"

He shakes his head. "Not quite. It's at the center."

As we approach, I take in the silhouettes of several transports slowing to a crawl, though we keep our pace.

A voice resounds through the cabin. "If Your

Graces would prepare for landing, we're cleared to dock."

"Hold on," says the duke. "Landing can get bumpy."

That's all the warning I get before my stomach drops with the change of altitude.

I choose to sit, though I remain close to the window.

We fly under a thick layer of clouds so opaque I consider that they might have been designed to keep the view obscured.

Then I see it.

Made of a dark metal I can't identify at this distance, the colossal quadrangular castle is curtained by high walls and towers so high I can't see the bottom at first.

All around us, the five mountains stand proud, cutting off the access to this place by any means other than air.

I understand now the choice of location: this place is a natural fortress.

When we're much closer to the ground, my eyes take in the strange shapes at the center of the castle. Rectangles and squares, circles and long alleys.

I take the construction for a sort of city, at first, but the walls are too thin for a building.

I understand what I'm looking at only instants before we land.

A complex labyrinth, made of metallic walls and filled with greenery, water ponds, even a beach.

It's an oddity in this place, given how everything else is covered in ice, the castle included.

To my surprise, we land over the top of the maze.

The doors of the hovercraft open the moment we touch down, and two men in green and black rush in, bowing so low their faces almost kiss the flooring.

A stout common man in a fur jacket walks in, standing so straight he could snap in two. "Your Grace, welcome to Whyte Fort. We trust you had a pleasant journey? Your rooms have been prepared. If you would..."

I'm the first to race out of the transport, eager to understand what I've been seeing.

I soon understand my mistake, and turn back, closing the door for good measure. The very air attempted to kill me on the spot.

"Helyn, your coat!"

I'm so cold.

We're at the end of the summer, and I've never been as freezing in my entire life, though I must have spent less than two seconds outside.

My mother joins me and wraps the wool coat I reluctantly borrowed from her back in town. I'm glad I let her talk me into it. I might have lost a limb if I'd come with the flimsy jacket I intended to wear.

To my surprise, as I thrust my arms into the sleeves, my body ceases shaking. The material must be enchanted.

My second attempt at exiting the vehicle is more successful.

I fear my face and legs might suffer, but whatever

the coat is made of, it protects my entire body from the harsh elements. I can still feel the icy air, but it's not as overwhelming.

I can't believe the coldbloods can bear this temperature in nothing but blazers.

Under my feet, the floor is made of a thick, transparent layer, allowing a perfect view of the maze below.

That explains the forest and lakes. The labyrinth is indoors, protected from the elements, though its ceiling lets in the light.

"Formidable, is it not?" the duke asks over the constant hum of engines outside.

Dozens of crafts are in line to land and pass through security. We were rushed through it, but everyone else is waiting high in the air. There must be a hierarchy to the order of arrivals.

"That's not the word I would have used," I try to say, but when I speak, my teeth chatter so much I'm not sure he can comprehend me.

My body's not recovered from its first encounter with the Ravelyn air.

The duke, like the servants, and even the common attaché, seems perfectly comfortable. "Yes, it's cold, ugly, and miserable," he sums up accurately. "But it's also safe. We moved the royal court here after the last king was killed."

Everyone knows the Devar family was massacred fifteen years ago. I was only four at the time, but even I remember the stunned horror that filled the world at the news.

My memories of the event were remote and vague, as it happened when I was so young, but after all of my research this week, I know the king, his four wives and the seven women in his harem were killed, then piled up and burned. The children hadn't been spared, leaving only one survivor: Zale.

I can't imagine the trauma, but I hate him all the same. I'm not about to compare my ordeals to his, but I had a shitty childhood, and I don't use it as an excuse to be a tyrant.

We cross the clear courtyard and progress through black, sculpted doors, entering a great hall of silver walls, supported by onyx column so high I hurt my neck when I tilt my head back to try to see the vaulted painted ceiling.

Blissful warmth engulfs me and I sigh in contentment.

Now I'm no longer at risk for frostbite, I can admit that the inside of the castle is beautiful, in a frosty, forbidding way. Quite perfect for its king.

"The court used to be in held in the Black Keep. It's farther north, where the temperatures are so extreme only coldbloods can survive."

I can't imagine a place colder than this. I don't think I could survive for a full minute out of doors here without my coat.

"And commons live in this country?" I muse, baffled, though I know the answer: the population is half common, half demi, which makes Ravelyn the realm with the highest percentage of magik users. Now I know why.

The duke leads us through halls so tall and vast I wonder if this place was built for men or giants. We do come across courtiers and servants, many of them pale, blond, and long-limbed. They bolt out of the way, with nods and curtsies we don't return.

"Where are we going?"

"I have apartments here—several rooms, close to the heart of the palace, so it'll be a short walk to the throne room, where we're expected in about an hour. You ladies can refresh and I can catch up on some paperwork."

I let him lead the way, relieved I didn't attempt to make my own way.

Though I can hardly trust a man who chose to marry my mother, or Neleda herself, I'm glad of their company today.

This place is a beautiful, austere nightmare, and I can't imagine venturing here alone.

CHAPTER TWENTY
A TASTE OF TORMENT

The floor vibrates under the ruckus of the blithe dances, and the air is thick with the stench of wine. This feast alone should be enough to sate the growing need inside me, but I barely hear, smell and see any of the merriments.

The beast I harbor is waiting for one specific delicacy. I'll take her pain and misery over the decadence of the Whyte Fort.

Helyn is late, disrespectful vixen that she is, and I'm delighted by it. Every second she makes me wait for her is a moment I'll make her pay for.

Adelaid rushes up the seven steps leading to my dais and without so much as a curtsy or a word of greeting, grasps both of my hands in hers, pouting. "Why won't you join me for a spin?"

I excuse her blatant discourtesy only because it is Lughnasadh, a day of sin. And she does have cause for such presumption. I have celebrated many a festival with her, and her sister, and her cousin, and each of her friends. The young ladies and gentlemen of this court have made themselves available to their king, and I've tasted almost every one of them in turn.

I'll taste more, just as soon as I've enjoyed the main entertainment of the night: a lesson in humiliation.

I'm jonesing to see Helyn break under the trial I've planned for her.

"Later," I tell the enthusiastic beauty, withdrawing my grasp.

I mean it. For tonight's occasion, she braided her silky black locks with straw, holding it up with a broach shaped like a corn doll. Stunning as ever, Adelaid stands out as the comeliest in a sea of similar faces.

For now, I have little interest in anyone who isn't Helyn Stovrj.

"Dance for your king, sweetling."

She beams, taking the sobriquet as a sign of affection. I don't feel much for the girl, but I let her assume otherwise.

Adelaid Gyrth is the granddaughter of an earl of Flaur, and boasts a rich coldblood father. As well as having a suitable lineage, she also happens to be the most desirable lady in my court, which has allowed her to think she and I might have more than the occasional tumble. She might be right. When my mind turns to the matter of heirs and succession, her name will be somewhere around the top of my list of potential partners.

She's also ruthless and petty, but such attributes don't concern me.

Adelaid is only halfway down to the dance floor when my gaze lifts of its own volition, and falls on *her*.

My fingers find the armrest and dig into the hard stone. The slow rhythm of my heartbeat all but stops as the rest of the crowd disappears.

How dare she, I want to scream. Demand an explanation, an apology.

The more accurate question ought to be how *could* she, Helyn Stovrj, common worm of the streets of Magnapolis, stand above my court.

I take her appearance for what it is: an affront.

Helyn's breezy gown flows, fluid, the translucent muslin caressing her skin at every step. The shape of her leg is discernible through the almost see-through black fabric pooling at her feet, though at her thighs, a layer of green velvet obscures the view, highlighting the shape of her hips. It gathers at her slim waist and crosses over her breasts, mingled with streaks of silver.

As she approaches, I note that the velvet's studded with green sapphires and the silver at her neckline is shaped like a raven in flight.

She's wearing the colors of Ravelyn, as if she belongs here. A queen wouldn't have looked prouder of her kingdom than this presumptuous, disrespectful wench.

The worst is her hair. What in the name of the shade has she done to her hair? Instead of flying all over the place, aimless and chaotic, it falls in soft, defined burnished copper curls.

Straining to contain my ire, I suck in a steadying

breath before she reaches the dais, only then noticing that all move to let her pass.

I could lie to myself and say they're giving way to my regent, who walks five feet behind her, his new wife's hand in his, but I know better. My court is parting for her.

Her!

No one dances, or drink, or talks, staring at the common girl in her silly costume, and at me. They're watching my reaction like vultures circling in search of a weakness. I have to contain my desire to cross the space between us and wrap my hands around her pretty neck. I am king, and I will not let anyone see her get under my skin.

Helyn reaches the step of the dais and has the audacity to walk up, one step, then another, and the next.

She stops to look over me, as if I were beneath her, as if she is the one in charge here. "Well, you summoned. Here I am."

I'm going to delight in her fall from this imaginary grace she claims.

"Here you are." I let a slow smile spread over my face as I stand. "'My court, Lady Helyn, heir to the duke of Elandheart." I don't need to raise my voice in the stunned silence.

I magnanimously extend my hand, gesturing for her to take it. She hesitates, but lifts hers to mine.

I barely touch her fingertips, but their warmth doesn't escape me.

"Now, some of you may wonder whether a girl

born in the gutter of a polluted mainland city could one day rule one of our strongest territories," I continue evenly. "I too have formed such a concern."

Helyn has the audacity to grasp my palm in warning, her fist tight over mine.

My grin broadens. "Lords and ladies, gentlemen and artists, friends and foes, saints..." I look over at Helyn. "And whores."

Hatred shines in her eyes, so intense it's palpable.

The gods were wise not to bless such a spirit with magik. With a will like hers, she could have toppled kingdoms.

"I challenge the future duchess to roam the maze."

The crowd explodes, screams, applauds.

I haven't opened the maze once in the fifteen years of my reign, yet I cannot think of a punishment more fitting.

The silver labyrinth was designed as a respite for my ancestor, the halfblood king who conquered both islands, who stole the strongest woman of Xhera and made her his queen. To anyone but those of my blood, this place is torment, an ever-changing personal nightmare.

"And what are the stakes?" My regent's glaring at me, his anger barely concealed.

She's his stepdaughter, and he doesn't appreciate my calling her out.

It's about time he learns I am king.

"For getting out of the maze?" I chuckle. "Well, the crown jewels are at the center. It's the lady's choice."

No one is expected to solve the maze; the challenge is to endure as long as possible.

"No one gets that far," Salvar Rhodes seethes. "It is custom to provide a boon for those who remain inside for a determined amount of time, your highness."

True, but she won't last ten minutes before begging to be rescued, and my court will see her for what she is.

"Sal, Sal. You drive a hard bargain. Say your girl stays an hour, she will be honored above anyone in the court. Two, and she may have her weight in gold. If she stays till dawn," I don't try to contain my laughter, "I'll make her queen."

CHAPTER TWENTY-ONE
INTO THE FIRE

The maze.

There is no doubt in my mind that he's referring to the complex, immense construction I was so taken with when we arrived. I'd wanted to see it closer then. Now, with Zale standing proud, victorious, and cruel, I'm nervous about getting that wish fulfilled.

I read nothing of a maze in my research about Ravelyn, which unsettles me further. I rarely go into any situation without thorough preparation.

The king's triumphant smirk says it all. I am in too far over my head. Not only am I expected to fail, I'm also likely to suffer.

There's something unsettling in seeing Zale like this; he wears only slacks and a shirt open to almost his navel, even more casual than his usual debonair attire, but I don't miss the silver crown on his messy white-blond hair, or the large signet ring at his right hand.

"Well, if she gets to compete for the crown, so

should I!" someone screams, interrupting my glaring at Zale.

He breaks eye contact first, looking over at a woman at the front of the crowd, close to the platform holding his marbled stone throne.

I'm surprised to recognize Adelaid from alchemy, dressed in a form-fitting white gown with a deep plunge at the front and back.

Murmurs of agreement cross the court, though no one dares to express themselves as brazenly.

Zale is unbothered. "By all means, you may all enter the maze, and the stakes remain the same."

If Zale trusts none of the magik wielders here could hope to remain a single hour, though they're familiar with this place, the maze is more dangerous than I can dream.

The king lets go of my hand to walk through the great hall. After seven strides, he looks back. "Well? Any day now."

I bite my lip, and reluctantly follow him out of the hall, trailed by the rest of the court.

We reach a grand staircase leading upward and splitting into two branches that head down, into an empty darkness.

I already regret my choice of clothing. My gown drops to the floor; carefully, I walk down the flight of stairs, until we reach the most imposing sets of doors I've ever beheld.

Identical ugly faces frozen in screams greet us at eye level on either side of the scarlet double doors, surrounded by snakes and spiders as large as dogs. I survey the horrible art, distinguishing scarabs and poisonous plants, giant worms and wasps in the carvings.

"The doors will open on the hour. There are four entries: green, black, red, and white doors. You may exit through whichever one you'd like except this one." Zale gestures to the red monstrosity. "Should you wish to get out of the maze at any time, scream my name and you'll be rescued."

His amused smirk is directed toward me, but a black-haired young girl, perhaps sixteen at most, clears her throat. "Is there anything dangerous in there?"

"Only your mind." Zale doesn't bother to glance at her. "The contestant may remain here, the rest of us can watch the bailey from the battlements. Who cares to place a wager on who will remain the longest?"

With those parting words, he returns to the stairs ahead of his flock, leaving me with seven women who all glower at me.

The young brunette who was sensible enough to ask Zale about the danger has remained behind, and she's the first to approach me. "I don't believe we've been introduced. I'm Pava Mayor."

"Hel," I say, forcing a smile.

I pity her. What could possess her to submit herself to whatever torture the king has in store for us? And if by some sort of miracle, she lasts until morning, she's far too young to bear the mantle of queen of anything.

"Like, a circle of hell?"

I shrug. "It's Helyn, but that was also my grandma's name. She went by Lyn, and I claimed Hel."

"Nice! I don't know any Hels, and there are plenty of Pavas." Then she's done with polite conversation, jumping to the meat. "How do you know the king?"

I'll wager it's the burning question on everyone's lips right now. Some misguided fools might have taken his attention for regard, though it's likely most saw right through his anger and hatred toward me. Either way, they want the gossip.

I opt to tell her the truth. "I don't."

There's almost nothing I know about Zale Devar, other than the fact that he chose to hate me at first glance, and I return his distaste.

She doesn't let my nonanswer deter her. "He's never sent anyone to the maze—not once. The old king used to make a dozen people walk through it every week. And now he makes you take the trial, and offers his hand if you manage it?" She tilts her head, hands on her hips, everything about her stance demanding an answer.

I chuckle. She's ridiculously direct. "We met in Magnapolis—at Five." I don't bother to say a word about our first encounter in the garden. "He's not fond of the fact that I'm at the top of the classes we have in common."

Her eyes grow impossibly wide. "But he's a genius."

I shrug, getting irritated now. "I'm good at studying."

I have noticed that Zale seems to score almost as high as me, when he's entirely relaxed, casual. A genius, he may well be, to my frustration.

Adelaid sneers. "Hm. Right. You're top of our year because of skills. Everyone knows your whore of a mother and the duke pay your way."

I don't bother to point out how ridiculous the notion that my family could bribe the professors or administration with more money than their king could. In fact, I ignore her entirely, which only serves to enrage her.

"Zale hates her. She's common, and she doesn't know her place."

"I did notice that you and your ridiculous king are racist," I admit with a conciliatory nod. "It sounds like your problem, not mine."

Her jaw falls.

"Who can blame him?" one of the women, older than us and elegant in a puffy gown, says. Everyone's abandoned the appearance of indifference, openly eavesdropping on our conversation. "After what happened to his family, I'd keep my circle closed, too."

I frown. "Just because they were killed doesn't justify his hating the greater part of the population."

Pava frowns, and some of the girls exchange a confused look.

"They weren't just killed," Adelaid spits out. "They were drugged at dinner, then dragged into the musical hall and tortured when they couldn't move. The women and children were raped, the men, mutilated, slowly cut and drained of their blood. Only then did the monsters pile them up and burn them, some of them alive."

My stomach sinks at the picture she describes.

"Zale still has the scars, you know. One on his chest, right under his heart, and several on his back, from the lashes he took. And all of that was done by common folk, unhappy about their station in our world. People like you."

My mouth open and closes. I'm too nauseous to attempt making my point at first. "A handful of crazies doesn't define my entire race—just like I wouldn't judge all demis simply because you are a raving bitch."

Even as I say the word, I wonder how true they are.

I certainly don't open up to demis easily, and I'm reluctant to accept magiks because her kind has taken advantage of mine for centuries.

What would I be like if a demi had killed everyone I loved, and right in front of me? If what she says is true, Zale witnessed his family's demise. He lived through it and somehow survived.

I have a thousand questions I can't ask, and the details were never released to the public. I would have remembered the poor boy who lived through the horrors who broke the rest of his line.

I remember everything, but this would have stayed anchored at the forefront of my mind.

I used to think his past didn't even begin to justify his prejudice, but now, I'm not so sure. I didn't imagine anything so grim and violent.

Before anyone can think of another word to throw at one another, the red doors swing wide with a plaintive wail, opening the entrance of the maze.

Beyond the doors, two tall brushed silver walls stand proudly, some ten yards apart, and I can't see anything on the horizon, other than blinding light.

It makes no sense. It's the middle of the night, on the twenty-eighth hour, and I know for a fact the sky ought to be dark, but this place feels like a warm, sunny afternoon in my city.

We walk together as one, wordlessly, Adelaid leading our procession.

I purposely take my time, falling toward the back. My dress brushes the sanded floor, and I wince at the thought of damaging the silk, so I bend down, gather the edges in my hand, and tie them at my hip, revealing the length of my left leg, but I doubt any of the girls will mind seeing a little skin.

When my gaze lifts forward again, they've all disappeared, and instead of a large, nondescript alley surrounded by strange wall, I'm standing in Glitter Lane. Or rather, what Glitter Lane would have looked like, scrubbed clean and void of all merchants, all inhabitants.

"Is there anything dangerous in there?"

"Only your mind."

This can't be good.

CHAPTER TWENTY-TWO

WAKING NIGHTMARES

I n all my years as king, never have I pleased the court as much as I did by reopening the maze. With very little alcohol, and no other entertainment, my subjects are delighted, gleefully squirming and pointing and screaming at the girls making their way into their deepest fears, their sorrowful memories, and worst of all, their hidden desires.

The Balfur girl lasts fifteen minutes at most, barely making it out of the first path, but she's too sweet for these games. She screams my name, and I send the royal guard to retrieve her.

They follow each girl, walking through the walls, so her rescue's almost immediate.

I've instructed them to take their time during Helyn's turn. They can take a coffee break, maybe make a sandwich before getting her out.

My eyes stay glued to the redhead as she bends to lift her skirts, to the delight of the folk of my court cheering her on. She's barely showing any skin, but they gawk all the same.

Done with her gown, she walks slowly, carefully, while I watch Adelaid wail and run wildly, glancing behind her shoulder then screaming at the top of her lungs.

I wonder what Helyn sees. I wonder why she isn't fighting it.

Nomena Dayn crawls on all fours, knocking the sanded ground every now and then.

Seven of them make it out of the first alley, two turning right, and five left.

There isn't a right or wrong path through the maze, as there are four entrances, but all paths lead to the center of the maze first.

Helyn has chosen to turn right. She's still slow and careful, but not nearly as affected as the rest of them, to my frustration.

She was supposed to be out already. She should be screaming like Adelaid, or peeing herself like the baron's daughter who begs off next.

Helyn keeps walking. She takes another right, and at first, I assume she's of the school who believe mazes ought to be solved by always taking the same turn. At least three women seem to harbor that misconception. When she reaches the third turn, Helyn takes an unexpected left.

I watch in rapture as she suddenly bends to a crouch, just like she did the very moment I met her for the first time. Then she leaps to the nearest hard wall.

I want to think she's gone mad like everyone who

remains. I want to see her break. That was the entire point of bringing her in to my domain, my control. I want to show her I can crush her spirit into my grasp. She's nothing exceptional. Just a common girl.

"Is she climbing the vines?" I hear one of my courtiers muse.

"How is she even seeing them?" another counters.

Both excellent questions.

My attention entirely focused on the girl who should have screamed my name ten times already, I lean forward in my box and watch.

That's when I understand.

She isn't seeing anything.

Oh, the cruel, sadistic, heartless monster!

I'll strangle Zale the next chance I get.

I didn't understand at first, but the lull of the familiar hums, the comfortable scents and voices around me felt wrong.

Then I saw him. A little boy I used to play catch with as a child. He froze one harsh winter after his parents disappeared. "Come play with me, Helyn. Why can't you join me?"

By the time I saw Grandma Lyn's smiling face and heard her rough, broken voice, I expected her.

It hurt all the same, like my heart was ripping in two.

"I never thought you'd let her in. You're better than

that. You're better than her. How could you forgive Neleda after everything she did to you? To me? You're betraying yourself. You're betraying my memory."

Each word feels like a dagger thrown directly at my heart.

"You left the lane. You left me. What do I have, now? Nothing. This is hell."

I can't tune out her voice, but at least, I shut my eyes to stop seeing my grandmother's heartbroken face as she crumbles to the floor.

That isn't Lyn Stovrj. She was strong and she would have commended me for taking what I can from Neleda. This shadow is just my fears, my doubts, reflected back at me to control my mind.

Knowledge is power. My grandmother believed it, and so do I.

Settling in a crouch to rest and think, I run through what I know. I am in a maze that attempts to trick my mind into seeing something else entirely, but its walls, its paths, are a concrete thing.

The walls.

I looked at these walls from above. My eyes surveyed almost it eagerly, and whatever I see, I remember.

I force myself to focus and visualize each shape, the squares and rectangles, the sandy beaches, the pond, and at the middle of it all, a circular atrium.

I rerun through my path in this castle. The duke took us straight toward the sunset. Inside the castle, we took three lefts, a right, walked forward again...

I take my time, forcing Grandma Lyn's voice to the

background. I place the throne room, the staircase, and finally, my red door on the other side.

My mind tries to reconcile all those bits of information with the maze I saw from above, but I fail. I can't quite decide which direction I'm facing.

But I remember the atrium. Getting out of here from the center should be doable. All I have to be careful of is not to turn back toward the same door.

"I thought you were going to come back to us," Alva cries. "Hang out with us. You never did, Hel. Not once. You think you're better than us, now that you're attending that school, wearing fancy clothes, and driving a car you could have sold to save a hundred kids in the lanes. You're one of them."

Enough of this already.

I need to get to the center of the maze, and I know the fastest way to do so.

I open my eyes, long enough to take in my surroundings, pointedly ignoring the distorted faces surrounding me.

That's when I spot it. A tree branch over the top of a merchant's sign, that shouldn't have been here. Flora's rare and memorable on the lane. Refusing to question myself, I leap away from the crowd of harpies. At worst, I'll hit a wall. It wouldn't be the first time.

My fingers catch on a sinuous branch and I grin, closing my deceitful eyes. Relying on my sense of touch over everything else, I climb higher and higher, remembering how thick the trees had seemed from above.

I refuse to consider the possibility of falling. I

haven't taken a fall since I was twelve, and it's not about to start now, for the entertainment of his highness, the king of jerks.

At long last, my hand scrapes against a cold, unfamiliar surface that feels nothing like the walls of my city. I lift myself up to the top of the wall, and finally dare to open my eyes.

I'm no longer in the undercity, but atop a thick, metallic platform, surveying the labyrinth from above.

I lift my gaze to the clear glass ceiling above, and almost immediately spot the king, standing in the battlement, eyes on me. He's too far for me to see his expression, but I'd bet he isn't pleased.

I grin. It's not my fault if he didn't bother to specify rules.

I shoot him my middle finger, and start to tread along the walls.

CHAPTER TWENTY-THREE
THE HEART OF THE MAZE

I spot the green door, and I could have headed right for it, but now that I no longer have to endure all the voices of my regrets, I opt to aim higher.

What was it the king had said? If I solved the maze, I could take one of his crown jewels from its center.

Maybe I should take the high road and just get out of here. That would be enough in the way of retribution. It doesn't feel like enough, though. He attempted to humiliate me, and I can turn it around on him.

"Say your girl stays an hour, she will be honored above anyone in the court. Two, and she may have her weight in gold. If she stays till dawn, I'll make her queen."

I grin. I could stay right here for hours on end, waiting for the rise of dawn and have his crown for my efforts.

I have no desire to submit myself to his company

for the rest of my days, but I imagine how ruffled he'll feel, knowing I had that option and chose to walk away.

Everything else he offered, I'll take.

I haven't paid attention to the time, but I've spent at least one hour here, and getting to the center of the maze and back ought to take one more. I only wish I weighed more, because the lanes are about to receive a hundred and twenty pounds of gold.

Glancing down to the path as I walk, I spot Adelaid curled up on the floor, crying, and I try to feel bad, but fail in that endeavor. She could always call for help.

It takes a while to reach the large, open circle, but I know I'm in the right place when I spot the willow tree planted at the very center, right in front of a glittering river so crystal clear it seems right out of a dream. Like everything else here. Good dream, bad dream, it's all just a side of the same coin.

Bracing myself for more onslaught, I climb down from the closest turn.

I expect the voices and visions to come back, so I close my eyes, but seconds pass and there's nothing but a soft breeze, the smell of lavender, and the sound of mating crickets chirping in the background.

Frowning, I advance into the clearing toward the tree.

"It is considered polite to curtsy in the presence of kings, you know."

I come to a stop, both confused and wary, because I recognize that voice.

His.

The maze isn't done with its tricks yet.

Zale appears in front of me, smirking as usual, though instead of being almost white, his hair's black and his eyes, amber. His skin seems warm and inviting to the touch.

As much as I hate, hate, hate the boy I know, this one makes my heartbeat skip and my skin flush.

This perhaps is the worst trick the maze threw at me.

"Keep dreaming, asshole."

He laughs, folding in two.

"Ah. That mouth on you. You'll do quite well here. The north is harsh and needs resilient souls." The strange, cordial Zale extends his hand to mine.

I stare at it like it might bite me. "I'm good, thanks."

He rolls his eyes. "Gosh, you're a hard nut. Go on by yourself if you must. You'll find the jewels at the base of the tree. Take whatever you'd like, as the boy offered."

"The boy," I repeat. "Don't you mean you?"

Zale wrinkles his nose. "By all hells, no. I'm not nearly as broody."

"You are," a singsong feminine voice laughs, though I can't tell where it comes from, and I certainly can't see anyone else in the plain.

"Am not." Zale stomps his foot and laughs, more openly than I'd ever thought possible.

I'm so glad I haven't met this version of him. He's the kind of man women lose their minds for, and he'd happily chuckle while eating their beating hearts.

"What are you?" I asked, confused and wary.

I should have returned directly to the door.

"A memory, if you will. This place was built to preserve long-lost echoes, so that I could remember the good days, after losing so many of my loved ones." His face falls, shedding all humor, and I want to run at what I see.

He's the shade inside Zale, the nightmare everyone ought to fear.

"Over time, after I was gone, my spell decayed and became this perverse thing very few people can withstand." He licks his lip. "No one, in fact, until you. I am glad to have met you, Helyn. You give an old soul hope for his kingdom."

Old.

This boy looks every bit like Zale, his features all the same, just in darker shades, but their feel is completely different. I finally understand I'm not looking at the current king of Ravelyn.

"You're Tryn. Tryn Du Var."

He grimaces. "Duval, please. My mother was a weak fool who disowned and banished me the moment she realized I was more powerful than she."

Tryn Duval. The monster who conquered two islands of powerful misfits, and the high fae queen of crows. The first king of Ravelyn. "So you...condensed her name? Way to be rebellious."

"Ha!" I've never seen a smile so genuine on Zale's face. I'm disturbed by how attractive that makes him. "You're one to talk, *Hel*."

A chuckle crawls up in spite of myself. "Point taken. You're just supposed to be smarter than me. You're a great king."

He shrugs. "Hardly. I was twenty, and my choices were conquer or die. I merely opted for the path that kept my head upon my neck. History has a way of embellishing everything."

His apparent humility disarms me. "Aren't you the son of the god king of shade?"

He's supposed to be greater, wilder, and certainly more evil.

Tryn grins. "I like you." He tilts his chin forward, to the willow tree. "Take the dagger. It'll serve you better than any crown."

I don't miss the fact that he never answered me.

He starts to fade, and panic grips me all of a sudden. I don't think I can let him go. "Wait!"

The boy reappears, to my left side this time, hovering inches off the ground. "Yes?"

I clear my throat, trying to cut to the heart, and find the important thing out of the thousand questions crossing my mind right now. Who else has had a chance to commune with Tryn Duval these last centuries?

I choose to go for self-preservation, asking the one thing that matters. "What is he? Zale. You were... feeding on blood, and your partner, she was fae, right? What does that make him?"

I need to understand that much in order to know how to resist his control.

Knowledge is power.

"Other than a spoiled brat?"

I decide I like Tryn.

"Diana fed on an array of merriments, and I, on

blood. Our descendants can survive on either." He grins. "Mostly, they chose the former."

I blink in confusion. "Uh?"

"Sex, sweetling," the olden king spells out for me with an eye roll so utterly like his descendant's. "Zale feeds on sex. Or pleasure. Or terror, if he's in the mood." His lips extend over his sharp white teeth. "But if he feels like it, he can also survive on blood."

CHAPTER TWENTY-FOUR

THROUGH THE MIRROR

As the ghost of the old king disappears for good, I decide I should have asked for a list of potential weaknesses, though I doubt he would have shared as much. Zale is his however-many-greats-grandson, after all.

It's a wonder Tryn told me as much as he did. He must have been incredibly bored alone in the maze for hundreds of years, and in want of conversation.

I cross the river to the willow, half expecting a monster to leap out of the surface and drag me underwater, or another ghost to spook me. Nothing of the sort occurs, and as promised, I find a pile of shining jewels at the base of the tree. Necklaces with precious stone hearts as wide as both fists, gold rings with diamonds, and so many crowns, diadems, even a scepter.

There also are a number of weapons, all too impractical to serve much purpose other than ceremonial posturing. A long broadsword with a hilt the size of an eggplant stands out, its scabbard shining like a thousand stars. The whole thing must weigh a hundred pounds.

Though the crown jewels have been piled up like discarded toys, every item seems just as sharp, shiny, and beautiful as the day they were forged. There must be some magiks at work, keeping everything safe from rust and dust.

It takes a while to spot the dagger—the only one I can see in the pile of treasures. Barely longer than my hand, the blade's made of a black metal. I notice its hilt, encrusted with large rubies. Taking it in my hand, I'm surprised to find it both light and comfortable.

If not for Tryn's guidance, I would have chosen a crown, as that's likely the option Zale would dislike the most. I know better than to ignore the advice of a ghost king, though. Incurring his wrath would be unwise, and one Duval enemy is already more than I can chew. Plus, he's right. This is perhaps the only thing in this stack that could be of any use.

I don't usually carry a weapon, unlike Alva and Khel, relying on my speed and ability to hide over my brawn, but this small thing is hardly more than a letter opener or a steak knife. And it's undeniably lovely.

Dagger in hand, I face the opposite direction from where I came from and hop on the vines, climbing back up to the top of the smooth, high walls.

I survey my surroundings, considering my position and what I've seen so far—I came from my left and spotted the green gates straight ahead.

Might as well explore the other side of the maze.

It's been a while since I've had a chance to stretch my muscles, and this almost feels like running on the rooftops of the lane, though the air's cleaner and the obstacles, much easier. And if I infuriate an arrogant king the longer I remain here? All the better.

I've traversed enough of the maze to reconcile my progress with the directions scorched in my mind from when I looked through the glass floor of the ward. I know where I am.

I could remain on the walls until I reach the black gate, but at the last turn, I opt to walk down to the ground one last time, counterintuitive as the action might seem.

I've read a book about psychology that delved into nightmares, into guilt and regrets, and after meeting Tryn's ghost, I'm confident I need to do this.

Earlier, I managed to get out because I told myself nothing I saw or heard was real. Now I know better. I start to understand the purpose of the maze, the reason why a man such as the first king of Ravelyn might have created this living nightmare.

This place was built to preserve long-lost echoes, so that I could remember the good days, after losing so many of my loved ones.

He told me the truth, at least partially, but the maze doesn't share good memories. It shares whatever baggage you take with you.

I've not even put one foot on the ground before Grandma Lyn appears, weeping and heartbroken.

Alva sniffles and shakes her head next to her. Khel averts his eyes, too disappointed to look straight at me.

And the poor boy whose name I can't even remember sits, head bowed in despair.

I approach Lyn tentatively, seriously hoping I'm not wrong. "I know what you are."

There were cues all along, but the biggest one was the voice I heard around Tryn—the girl who'd teased him about brooding just as much as Zale.

Everything I miss. Everything I desire. Everything I can't let go of.

Grandma Lyn's face ripples like water under the weight of a pebble and she morphs into an exact copy of myself, though she's wearing black gear and a hood low on her head.

My past smiles back at me and disappears. The boy stands up and a red ball appears in his hand. He bounces it on the ground, laughing as he vanishes behind a wall.

Alva and Khel start to bicker over the best place to get a pint of ale. "Come on, Hel. Let's go for a drink. You can be the designated sober idiot."

Khel shakes his head, exasperated with her, as they fade away.

Grandma Lyn's voice is the last thing I hear before the lane vanishes, giving way to the silvery walls.

"Leaving won't turn you into your mother. Nothing could. Let yourself move on, and the sky's the limit."

She's not real. Grandma Lyn has never said that to me, because she could never have seen where I would be after her death. She's an echo, just like Tryn. A ghost created by all of my memories of her. But I know without any doubt that if she'd been here right now, she would have said the exact same thing.

I cross the lane and breathe out, bracing myself. Strange that his nightmare of a maze wasn't as daunting as the prospect of returning to his court.

I push against the black gates.

⁕ ⁕ ⁕

Cheers erupt all around me, and unfamiliar arms wrap around mine, squeezing hard.

I freeze, unaccustomed to such enthusiasm, let alone from strangers. By the time the hugger withdraws, I see it's a warm-skinned girl in brown servant garb.

She isn't the only one: almost all of the crowd gathered here is too tanned and pink for the coldblood court.

Neleda and her husband fight their way to me.

"Bloody brilliant, that was," the duke says, stunned. "Not since the days of Tryn has anyone but a Duval walked through the maze without losing their mind. My daughter, the hero," he calls, encouraging the cheers.

I grimace at his effusion. "I'm just...highly logical?"

I can't really understand how no one figured out how to get out.

My mother grins proudly, and I don't bother to roll my eyes.

The servants scamper, but a number of common

courtiers and even some halfbloods trail us, still cheering, acclaiming my accomplishment. I can't say I mind. In fact, I would much prefer remaining right here with these strangers rather than returning to the great hall, but I let the duke drag me back up the stairs.

Time to face Zale Devar.

This round is mine, but he's not likely to accept my victory and let me get out of here unscathed.

CHAPTER TWENTY-FIVE

DANCE OF SNAKES

I leave the battlements and return to the throne room in silence, ignoring the dunces celebrating by my side.

What do they have to cheer for? The best of our ladies begged to be carried out of the maze in instants, and one common woman shamed them so badly I wouldn't show my face for the next hundred years in their stead.

Harl Greystone catches up to me and pats my back as though we're the best of friends. "You rascal. I understand why you took your time, after all. She's a wise choice."

I'm horrified to understand he's assuming I expected that Helyn would conquer the maze. He thinks I planned this, to make her win the heart of my court.

Yet what can I say—that she made a fool out of me and everyone else here?

"How's your wife?" I ask, concealing my irritation behind a smirk.

Harl is undeterred, but a little miffed. "Proud as a punch. She still boasts to all our friends about being singled out by the king, you know."

I give up in my endeavor to annoy him, resorting to speeding up to leave him behind.

Back in the great hall harboring my throne, I watch the excited crowd toast and cheer, exasperation rising at every moment I have to wait for the girl.

Again.

She finally appears at the head of a small procession, her dress still tied up at her hip, falling in waves down her left thigh.

This time, Helyn's entry isn't greeted by silence, but by roars.

Otto Nettlestein, my usually dignified advisor, rushes to her, screaming. "I bet on you! I bet you'd stay the longest! You won!"

He isn't the only one. Dukes and earls, princesses and greater ladies treat this common girl as though she just singlehandedly conquered an army of wraiths.

Helyn laps it all up, taking each praise, each familiar accolade by a crowd that would have loved nothing more than to see her fail only hours ago.

I watch, lounging on my throne, thoroughly ignored by my entire court. Each passing second increases my wrath.

I attempt to temper it. This night might not have turned out as I expected it to, but it was useful nonetheless. I understand the girl a lot better than I could have days ago, when I believed her to be nothing more or less than a thorn in my side.

She didn't solve the maze. She conquered it.

Once every so many centuries, the gods like to throw a wrench in the machine, so to speak. During the Dark Wars, it was Valina Frejr. A solitary dark witch shouldn't have determined the outcome of an all-out war between all of the mainland kingdoms, but she did, because the god of chaos planted a child who should have belonged on the eternal side of the map among us.

Who would have seen it coming? Plenty of people, I'd wager, had they been observant.

Helyn Stovrj isn't merely a common girl from the wrong side of the river.

I never bothered to see her as a real threat, but she can no longer be ignored. She's one enemy worthy of my personal attention. I get the feeling she might be my downfall unless I deal with her now, while she's still at my mercy, a subject of my court, under my rule.

I smirk as one devious idea comes to mind. Proud as she is, certain of her own worth, she'll hate every second of what I have in store.

The Silver Labyrinth may not have humiliated her, but this certainly will.

I stand, and my court barely notices me, but Helyn does. Dread flashes in her green eyes as she reads my expression.

I'm not done with her, and she knows it.

"Helyn of the house of Rhodes," I call.

Instead of falling into a respectful silence, the court screams her name over and over.

Helyn, Helyn, Helyn.

"You were promised your weight in gold and honor beyond any in this court."

In fact, I also dangled a crown, if she'd remained but a few hours longer. And she could have. The fact that she chose to walk out instead speaks volumes of both her character, and her distaste for me.

Which makes my plan all the more wicked.

"I am a man of my word. You'll have your gold, and as for honor..." My teeth flash as I pause. "You now stand above all but your king, as my first concubine."

Her jaw drops and wordless horror widens all her features. I wish I could immortalize her expression, and take out the picture to look at it every time I wish to be entertained.

Perhaps I'll have her painted just like that, and hang the art right here in the throne room.

"Welcome to my harem."

The court goes wild, losing whatever sense of decorum they might have left in the middle of the night on Lughnasadh. Many congratulate Helyn, some clap at me, and I hear toasts to wish her prosperity and fertility.

I only stare at her, relishing in her fear, panic, and hatred. Though she's at a distance, the taste of it feeds my soul more than any feast, orgy, or massacre ever could.

That's more like it.

If only I'd thought of this retribution sooner, I wouldn't have bothered with the maze. This is so much better.

I crook my finger to order her to my side.

I can practically see the wheels turning in her mind. She wonders how to get out of it. She can't, unless I release her. She wonders whether I'll force myself on her. I won't. I desire her dismay and submission, not her flesh.

She glances to her mother and stepfather, hoping for a lifeline neither of them extend. Neleda beams, delighted, and good old Sal pats her shoulder.

I didn't lie: the position I raised her to is an honor in the white court. An honor she abhors and resents, though I haven't even started tugging at her leash yet.

She joins me on the dais again, her cheeks red with fury and shame.

"I hate you," she whisper in a low breath.

I lean to her ear, making a show of pushing a long, sleek tress behind her shoulder. "Likewise, sweetling. And you're about to feel just how much."

She's but a breath away, so I don't miss the dilation of her pupils, or the small gasp of air from between her parted lips. Her gaze dips down to my mouth, and I know then what she's dreading. I almost give it to her. I almost kiss her to confirm her worst fears. But half of the game is her apprehension.

I return to my throne and recline on the uncomfortable seat.

"Well, are you waiting for a written invitation?"

She drags her feet to my side, mouth pinched. "Where am I supposed to sit?"

I weigh the deliciously demeaning possibilities, and

elect to make her pick her poison. "There's my lap or the floor at my feet, dearie. It's your call."

I could ingest the delicious taste of her fury from a distance, but now she's close, the waves of energy all but assault me, stronger than anything I've ever fed on, intoxicating and highly addictive.

As I knew she would, she chooses the floor, and spends the rest of tonight's feast where she belongs.

At my mercy.

CHAPTER TWENTY-SIX

THE FINE PRINT

This can't be happening. It can't. Zale Devar did not decree and announce to his entire realm that I am his designated slut. He didn't. I'm going to close my eyes and wake up in my bed. None of this is real.

"There must be something you can do about it," I hiss, back in the duke's suite.

I'm pacing the parlor back and forth, panic fighting anger for supremacy inside me.

My mother and Salvar Rhodes are equally baffled. They exchange a wordless stare, and he's the first to recover.

"It is an incredibly prestigious honor to be chosen by the king, Helyn. One he has not bestowed on any woman to date. You're now the head of this court, second only to the king himself. The only person higher in the hierarchy would be a wife."

Anger wins. "I don't care about hierarchy, or honor

and prestige." I could scream. "Can you get me out of this ridiculous, outdated, misogynistic mess or not?"

I didn't make waves in the throne room, because airing my laundry in front of a mob more likely to support him than me wouldn't be smart, but if Zale thinks for even a moment that I'll let him reduce me to his royal seed receptacle, he's even more insane than I thought him to be.

He made me sit at his feet on the cold floor for hours, and the court couldn't stop gushing about how lucky I was.

Lucky!

"Well," the duke starts, "women selected to be part of the king's harem can be released from their duty..." I sigh in relief before he finishes his sentence. "By the king."

I screech.

"I don't understand you, Helyn. Zale Devar is a handsome young man, rich beyond measure, influential, and he clearly cares for you," my mother reasons. Then she sighs. "But if your affections are engaged elsewhere, surely, His Highness will understand, and release you if you ask it of him."

She can't be this naive, can she?

"Zale," I hiss, "hates me. He hates me more than anyone or anything on this planet. In fact, Zale's hatred for me has only one equal, and that's my feeling toward him. The god of shade has never hated the goddess of light more than I detest him!"

My mother's speechless. She hasn't had the pleasure of witnessing one of my legendary fits of temper yet.

With her, so far, I've remained cold and impersonal. She's never been close enough to me to see me lose it like this, unlike Grandma Lyn, who typically just laughed at me and made me tea.

I miss her terribly all of a sudden.

"That's not the impression I had," the duke says diplomatically. "You seem perfectly civil to one another."

"Has no one ever told you about a thing called pretense? You're a politician, you should know what it's like!"

He winces. "All right, fair. Then, you think he chose you as a way to vex you."

"I know he did. If I were on fire, Zale wouldn't piss on me to put it out."

"All right, I get the picture." A chuckle escapes the duke. "Well, you may yet use the situation to your advantage."

Now he has my attention. "How so?"

He shrugs. "Well, a first concubine has rights as the head of the royal household. The king may ask for your company, and have you dressed a certain way..."

My jaw slacks at that news. "I don't see any advantage."

"What he cannot demand is your, ermm—" He glances at my mother. "Your attention."

"So, I'm now his slave, but that's good news because he can't force me to jump him?" I practically shriek, incapable of calming the anger rising again.

Truth be told, that is good news. I can't imagine

Zale would want me, but his desire to make me suffer might exceed his disgust for my common blood.

"No, of course not. The advantage is that he may not send you away. The only person in the world with that right would be his first wife, the queen. As he doesn't have one of those, you're his equal in the eyes of the court. At any time of your choosing, you may appear and demand to be seen."

My first instinct is to yell some more. Why would I want to spend more time with him? But I soon understand the duke's train of thought. "I could annoy him into letting me go free."

It's one thing for Zale to call me to him at times he'd find convenient in order to annoy me, but he would hate my invading his life under any other circumstances.

He inclines his head. "He might have picked you to displease you, but you do have the power to be as much of a nuisance to him as you wish."

I'm still nettled and on edge, but I do manage a fleeting, grateful smile for the duke, just as a knock startles us.

"Yes?" he calls imperiously.

Two rail-thin ladies, both white as a sheet and draped in identical gray frocks walk in, eyes lowered to the ground. "We're here to take Lady Helyn to her chamber, Your Graces."

"My chamber?" I snap, frothing at the mouth like an enraged dragon.

I feel bad when the girls shift nervously. It's not their fault I'm in this mess. It's his.

"Am I not returning to the city with you?"

The duke has the sense to wince. "Not if the king wants you to remain with him."

Oh, bollocks.

I am housed in a richly furnished, large room of white walls painted with thorns, completed by thick green velvet upholstery. It is fit for a queen, yet I sleep worse than I ever did on a hard pallet, half expecting Zale to walk in and demand salacious favors from his new whore.

The duke's words did reassure me, but I am still Zale Devar's concubine, and in the quiet of the night, that fact takes precedence over rationalizations. I keep my dagger close, and the king never comes.

In the morning, I wake to the sound of light footsteps approaching before my door opens. I have the ruby-studded hilt in my grasp in an instant.

"Oh, by the gods!" One of the two pale silver-haired maids jumps. "I'm sorry, ma'am, I'm here to draw your bath. I thought you might still be asleep."

I want to grunt and throw my head back on the pillow, but I couldn't sleep before her arrival. "My fault. I'm on edge." I sit up, setting my dagger back down on the feather mattress. "What was your name?"

I don't think I bothered to ask when she and her companion brought me here last night, frustrated and angry as I was, but it's certainly not my wish to anger servants. I relate to and like them much better than any of the grand titled folk. Not to mention, the two servants led the way yesterday and I don't have a hope in hell of finding anything without them. Trying to be nice won't hurt.

"Nissa, Your Grace."

"Enough with graces, I'm Hel." I get out of bed and follow her into an adjacent room. "Do you know what I'm supposed to do today, Nissa?"

"We're to dress you and take you down in three hours, you—" She catches herself. "Hel. The king requested your presence."

I'm sure he did.

The last time anyone washed me, I must have been three or four. At her behest, I let the cold-handed woman scrub my back as her coworker and sister, Lupa, kneads her talented finger into the sole of my foot. Most of my worries subside, clouded over by a shroud of blissful contentment.

For a time.

I know that's not likely to last.

"If your ladyship's ready, it's time to dress. We wouldn't want to be late for the king."

I groan, but keep my mouth shut and with a longing sigh, rise out of the water. Nissa hands me a flocculent dressing gown she warmed for me.

Wrapping it around my shoulders, I tell her honestly, "I want to kidnap you."

I'm rewarded by a sunny smile. "I am at Your Grace's disposal."

She's having a hard time using my name, and I've given up reminding her.

I never understood how anyone might wish to be waited on hand and foot as though they were incapable of caring for themselves, but in less than two hours of this, I'm getting used to it.

"I don't have any clothes except for what I wore yesterday," I realize.

"Oh, the king had a dress made overnight," the second servant, Lupa, says in a tone I'm certain she thinks is reassuring.

My stomach drops.

"How generous."

My trials at the white court are far from over.

CHAPTER TWENTY-SEVEN

PEARLS IN THE GARDEN

T he court rarely wakes before high noon on days after festivals, but after seven hours in my bed, I've not slept one wink. I give up, and take the chance moment of quasi-solitude to explore the archives kept in the royal library.

I'm shadowed by my guards, naturally, but their presence has been a constant in my life for long enough for me to completely ignore it. Besides, they're not the ones I aim to avoid.

No one will look for me for hours, and if they do, they won't come here, to the dreary, messy alcoves where our literature and documents are stored. Not when I have a brand-new concubine to warm my bed, in the eye of the court.

My father was never one for books, so he had the old library converted into a ballroom. Now, we keep the millions of ancient volumes in a dark and cold ancient hall, and spell them to withstand the damp. I make a mental note to tell the clerk to do something about the stench too. At a less unseemly hour, the room will no doubt be manned, and my every move watched.

I know exactly what I'm looking for.

Every time a lord or lady, great or small, enters any of the courts, their presence is recorded, and copies are sent to all of the royal halls. I look for a date marked in my brain in hot iron—Ostara, year 1404: the day my family was massacred.

I run through the list of names in attendance at the Black Keep, the house I grew up in, the one I intend to return to the moment I shake my regents loose.

Greystone was there, and Adler, and Rhodes, but so were most of the great lords, to celebrate the spring equinox. Coldbloods rarely decline an excuse for a party.

I frown as I read an unexpected name on the list. Valina Frejr.

What was the head of the Frejr clan doing here? She rarely ever leaves the Darklands.

I'll find out.

The list otherwise yields no surprises, no matter how long I stare at it, so I move on to the royal correspondences I can find from around that period. Boring missives of no import, talking of a land dispute in the southern isles, a shortage of wheat, and the increased tariffs on fish exports.

I'm getting tired, frustrated and the pressure at the back of my head doesn't stop.

I blow out the single candle at my desk and return to my apartment for a change of clothing and a rest.

It's almost midday, and my favorite toy is about to be delivered to me, wrapped in highly diverting packaging.

Rather than the great hall and its uncomfortable seating arrangements, I choose to hold court in the Little Garden, a domed atrium ordered by my great-grandmother, who'd been fond of roses. Supported by twelve rose pink pillars, overtaken by ivy, the gardens walls are covered in roses year around.

I sit by a fountain at its center on a red velvet reclining chaise, surrounded by a dozen courtiers who buzz in my ear like maddening little bees.

Adelaid has crawled as close as she dares, pressed up against the leg of my chair, not unlike Helyn yesterday.

"I just don't understand." She schools her voice into a plaintive moan, almost hiding the extent of her anger. "The common girl's not one of us. She's not even seen Ravelyn once before yesterday, and she'd die in minutes beyond the walls."

I ignore her, growing wary of the sound of her voice.

"She's very pretty," Aud Levendell quips.

Adelaid shoots her a glare.

"What? She is. All that bright hair and flushed skin."

"She's common," Adelaid counters.

"Well, she doesn't look it," another girl argues.

I bear their chatter without sending any of them to a dark dungeon, which ought to qualify me for sainthood.

The rest of my court lounges leisurely around the garden, divided in small circles established by either rank, friendships, age, or beauty.

Sadly, the closest thing I have to a friend in my kingdom is my advisor, and though good old Otto is in attendance, he chooses the company of Harl Greystone. Even if I could bear the ingrate's presence, his wife, the dark-haired beauty I sampled weeks ago, keeps sending me looks under her long lashes, so I know better than to make my way over there.

I'm waiting for superior entertainment.

When my patience is finally rewarded, I question every single choice I've made in the last thirty hours.

Helyn walks in alone today, dressed in the depraved, scandalous excuse for a dress I imagined for her. The first in a long list of torments I'm looking forward to inflicting.

I immediately regret my choice.

Entirely made of pearls strung in tight rows, the attire was executed to perfection by the royal tailor who used to dress my mother and the other concubines. I'm tempted to have him flogged all the same.

She wasn't supposed to look like this. Not only lewd, but also regal.

Powerful.

As instructed, Helyn is naked underneath the pearl gown, offering us all glimpses of her smooth skin between the neat, even, creamy beads.

She strolls down the row of courtiers with her head high and no one laughs, too taken by the sway of her hips or the curve of her heavy breasts. It is a bracing sight for any man—or woman—and to my disturbance, I am among them.

My jaw ticks in annoyance, because this is supposed to be a lesson, a punishment, and a humiliation designed for her, yet here I am, struggling to look away, my mind flooded with filth.

I might have regretted my misguided attempt at shaming her, but for the deep flush coloring her cheek.

She hates this.

At least I can savor that victory.

Adelaid inhales sharply. "She looks like a whore!"

"Watch your tongue or lose it," I snap.

She's right, and making her look like nothing short of a harlot was the entire point, but an insult to my concubine is a slight directed at me and no king will abide that.

I stand and cross the garden to meet her, before my knights and lords give into their desire to approach her, if only for a closer look, a touch, a word from her lips.

It wouldn't do to have to behead half my court.

My tongue runs over my teeth without my say-so as I approach, and I feel blood against my tongue. My teeth are sharper than I'd like.

She stops and snarls when we're a yard apart.

"If this isn't my concubine." I tilt my head back and let my eyes wander through the length of her dress. "You certainly look the part."

Oh, the fire in her green eyes! Her fury is worth my discomfort.

"Why are you submitting me to this?" She fumes between her teeth. "I've never done anything to you, not once."

I cant an eyebrow. "Nothing?"

"It's not my fault if I score higher than you in class! You want to beat me? Try studying more."

She truly believes she's here because of her alchemy score. Isn't that cute?

I cross the distance between us. "You're to hold Elandheart, half of the southern island of Ravelyn, a territory powerful enough to challenge the crown, though you have no understanding of our land, no respect for our customs, and show no desire to educate yourself. In the weeks since you were named heir, you did not bother to come to your country, to your land, until you were summoned here." I scoff. "You're a disgrace to our kingdom."

I mean every single word.

Ravelyn cannot afford to have someone like Helyn holding one of its three decisive seats. Making the court see her as nothing but a long pair of legs and heavy tits is for the good of the kingdom.

I've failed so far. Her performance in the labyrinth achieved the opposite outcome.

That said, I'm not torturing her solely because of politics.

I'm punishing Helyn Stovrj because nothing has given me greater pleasure, as far back as I can remember.

I wanted to play with her before I even saw her, from the first moment back in the duke's garden.

And from the sheer, defiant loathing in her eyes, I'd bet my crown she suspects as much.

CHAPTER TWENTY-EIGHT
FOLKS AND FOES

I've never worn anything as uncomfortable as this vulgar excuse for a dress. I cannot sit. I cannot shift one way or another, for fear of flashing my nipples to half the court. I certainly can't even dream of bending down to grab any of the refreshments presented on low coffee tables throughout the glass atrium.

Zale takes me for a stroll around the garden, ensuring I'm displayed before the wandering eyes of all his court.

I'm still reeling from his words, his accusations, partially because they're true and I can't deny they don't cast a flattering light on me.

I didn't bother to get to know the realm I'm now a part of. Why would I? I'll forever see myself as a child of Magnapolis, no matter what land my mother's husband rules.

But also reeling, because he's just using them as an

excuse, a shield. Zale *was* lying. He's torturing me because he loves it.

"Helyn, I don't believe you've met Sir Woodhouse."

Careful to never touch so much as an inch of my skin, keeping his fingers on the pearls covering my lower back, the king leads me to a man who looks around his age. Black haired, particularly handsome, he has acutely pretty features, almost effeminate. His pale skin distinguishes him as a coldblood, but the shape of his pupils, slanted like a cat's, make me think he may have folk blood mingled with it.

"Dayn is a knight of Elandheart. He's served the Rhodes family since the day of the duke's grandfather, isn't that right?"

The man's feline eyes remain locked on mine, not realizing that the king addressed him.

My jaw ticks. I know what Zale's doing. This specific knight will forever remember me as the barely dressed doll paraded here.

"Sir Woodhouse?"

With a start, he turns back to the king and clears his throat. "Apologies. Your Grace?"

"You've served house Rhodes for some time?"

"Three hundred years, Your Grace," he says proudly. "I am now a member of the duke's guard, though I am on leave."

"Helyn is the duke's stepdaughter. Perhaps you could tell her a little of the south she's never seen."

"With pleasure. The southern isle is much colder than the northern one, Lady Helyn, but it's also greener. Our forest extends for over a thousand miles, and the array of fauna would surprise you. It has been a refuge for the folk long before it ever became a prison for the mainland."

All of this is new to me, and I feel like the ignorant ingrate Zale accused me of being. Doubtless that was his aim.

"Over the last age, the folk and the coldbloods have lived in harmony, under the rule of house Rhodes and house Celian."

I don't think I've heard the second name. I'm itching to find the closest library, hating nothing more than ignorance.

"Do you like it there, Sir Woodhouse?" I ask politely.

"Very much. I was chosen as a squire to the duke's grandfather when I was as young as you, and in time, rose to knighthood. Merits are lauded as much as birth in the south," he adds with a pointed look around us.

That shouldn't surprise me. The duke did choose my mother, though she has no birthright at all. "I might just like it in the south."

I'm rewarded by a sunny grin and an elegant bow.

Zale takes my hand before either of us say another word. My head snaps to stare at him, and I frown, unsettled by the feel of his large and delicate palm against mine. His touch is icy, but if I'm startled, it's not by the cold as much as the jolt of awareness running through my entire body the moment our skin meets.

A shiver runs through my arm and I bristle.

Then he leads me away from Dayn Woodhouse

mid-conversation, like I am nothing but a slave to his whims.

I only think to withdraw my fingers when we've reached another man for him to parade me in front of.

I hate him so much it hurts.

Once he's ensured everyone here has gawked at my skin through the pearls from up close, he leads us to an informal deep red chaise, and lounges casually. I stand by his side, wondering how much longer I'll have to endure this penance for my imaginary crimes.

His bench is surrounded by pretty women, and I notice they all seem quite happy to sit by his feet as I did last night. I roll my eyes.

"Why won't you sit, dearie?" Zale purrs, bringing a cup of dark wine to his lips.

I may not be much of a drinker, but I could use a bottle or two right now. "Perhaps because you had me dressed in a row of necklaces."

Somehow, the other women, openly eavesdropping, find that hilarious.

"Did His Majesty choose this dress for you?" a brunette asks.

"It's glorious!" another says.

"And that hair! Is that your natural color?"

"Why don't we ask the king?" Adelaid Gyrth sneers. "I'm sure he found out if the carpet matches the drapes."

I'm so done with her nonsense. If we were in the lanes, I would have punched that dark haired dick in the boobs long ago. "Oh, he couldn't tell you," I purr, batting my lashes for her benefit. "I'm all bare below."

I'm gratified to see Zale choke on his drink and Adelaid gape.

The others are various shades of amused and shocked.

"That's beyond the pale!" the lady shouts, jumping to her feet. "Are we to bow to a vulgar cow?" She turns to look directly at her king and screams, "Did you hear what just came out of her mouth?"

I should leave well enough alone, but annoying her is too easy...and satisfying. "The king's quite fond of what I can do with my mouth."

Thanks to her ruckus, more courtiers approached, and they all laugh at her, surprising both me and her by taking my side.

Adelaid's blow is swift, if a little weak, striking right at my cheek.

I laugh, because this turn of events is a delight. Politics, court protocol, being chosen against my will for a role I'd never want, and stupid laws that prevent me from walking out? That's beyond my power.

Teaching Adelaid Gyrth isn't.

Without a thought for preserving my modesty in this joke of a dress, I lift it at my hips and lunge. I watch the brunette brace and gather her hands to her side, and I know she's about to use some magik.

The thing with witches is, they need precious seconds to prepare their spells. Facing another magik user, the delay might be irrelevant, but I don't have any energy to call upon but my own. Fast as I can, I dip low to the ground, swiping my leg out to hers. As she falls, I climb over her, one leather-clad foot pinning one of her hands.

I only glance to the king fleetingly, to check how he takes it. I don't want to lose my head for hitting a bitch.

Zale leans forward and smirks wordlessly.

Men. I chuff in contempt. Great or low, all of them enjoy watching a catfight.

When Adelaid tries to move, I press my knee harder into her chest. "Now that I have your attention, my lady, let me clarify one little thing. You're absolutely right. I am not one of you. Touch me, and I bite back."

She curls her lips. "You worthless cunt! How dare you touch me!"

"Adelaid." Zale's voice cuts through her bravado; she loses all fight as she turns her head to him, eyes wide. "Do not forget yourself. You are a guest under my roof. Your actions against my courtesan ought to have cost you your neck. I will spare it today. Do not expect my leniency to extend much further." He stands and extend his palm. "Helyn, you've had your fun."

I sigh, and let go of Adelaid's wrist first, then rise. "Spoilsport."

CHAPTER TWENTY-NINE

ANOTHER KIND OF WAR

This time I am prepared for Helyn's hand jerking my core the moment I take it, though I still don't fully comprehend what she is.

I should have her sent to a lab and dissected, to study every cell.

"Who was your father?" I ask her as we leave the garden.

She chooses to frustrate me, shrugging her shoulders and giving no answer. Then I remember her mother mentioning being assaulted by a random soldier, and it dawns on me that she might not know. "Have you had your blood tested?" I push.

"Why?" she snarls. "I can't put a demi bitch in her place if I only have common blood?"

Well, there is that. Weeks ago, I wouldn't have thought it possible, though Adelaid isn't known for her prowess as a fighter. But I'm not asking because she overpowered the other woman with ease. I'm asking because she's a puzzle with missing pieces. "Aren't you curious about your own nature?"

"No." She doesn't even hesitate. "Where are we going?"

"Wherever I want to take you."

In truth, I have no clue. I enjoyed our performance at court, but it was time for a respite from the toxicity and constant scrutiny. Usually, I would have left alone. I can't decide why I brought her with me. "Aren't you tired of fighting me at every turn?"

She sniggers, looking down at herself, before dragging her gaze back to me with a tilt of an eyebrow. She doesn't need to say a single word.

"It is a stunning gown, you must allow."

"You're telling the world I am your whore. I'll never grow tired of fighting you."

She's so proud, for a girl born in the gutter. Any woman in my court would sell their own parents to find themselves in her position, and she hates every second of it. "Being my courtesan is an honor."

"For an aimless, superficial, spoiled brat, maybe. I have other ambitions."

"What ambitions?" I wonder as we pass the armory.

Helyn snatches her hand back. "Let's not do this."

"What?"

"Pretend to be friends. In fact, there's no audience. Let's not speak at all."

Here she is again, the imposing beauty with her head up high, forgetting she isn't the one giving the orders here.

"You really do think highly of yourself."

"Why wouldn't I?" she challenges.

I lose it.

I don't know if it's her pride, her provocation, or the fact that I've been on edge since she first appeared today, but before I can stop myself, I have a fistful of her curls in one hand, one arm around her waist, and my mouth crashing to hers.

I've kissed a thousand women, more perhaps. Some were better than others, and all pale compared to Helyn Stovrj-Rhodes. Instead of a pleasant prelude to wilder games, taking Helyn's lips is a beginning and an end unto itself. I am careful at first, as if approaching a beast, unsure of whether it'll attempt to bite. Shivering, she remains still, frozen in place, shocked eyes widening as I press harder into her.

She gasps under my lips and I moan into the opening, needing more. Her soft mouth moves under mine and I lose all reason. I pin her to the closest flat surface, a window encasing the armor of an irrelevant king, hands gliding under the rows of pearls at her waist, desperate to feel, touch, more.

I despise myself for wanting this, wanting *her* more than anything, including the riches of the realm, the power of my crown.

I strain to remain in control, but when she returns my kiss, I abandon all hope. My tongue dancing against hers, I swallow every moan. The arms had remained at her sides raise and hook behind my neck, holding me closer.

I hiss.

I am a Devar, of the line of Tryn and his fairy

queen. I've always held influence over the desires of others. I've used that ability with care, never truly forcing myself on anyone. I don't need to. Men and women throw themselves at me wherever I go. In the game of seduction, I am the perfect predator and she should be the prey. This role reversal is disconcerting.

Grasping the extent of the power she holds over me in this moment is the only reason I manage to extricate myself from her, shaking with the effort it takes.

I let go and take a stumbling step back. Her mouth is stained deep red, bruised by my lips. She's panting, her chest rising and falling through the pearls. I notice the row over her nipples has shifted up, revealing the lobe of a dark areola.

I don't trust myself to speak—or move, for that matter.

"You're not supposed to do that," she whispers, lips trembling.

"Didn't you hear? You're my concubine, dearie." I'm relieved to sound like myself, callous and in control.

"The duke said you couldn't touch me unless I allowed it," she presses, anger firing in her deep blue eyes.

That's more like it. Like *us*.

I need her anger, and I ought to find mine.

"You allowed it." I force a chuckle that sounds fake to my ear, but she doesn't know me well enough to hear it. "You *liked* it. Interesting."

I make a good show of indifference, treating the entire debacle like an experiment well conducted.

I'm surprised she falls for it, clever as she is. Helyn groans in frustration, throwing her hands up, and takes off toward one of the exits.

My smile drops when she's no longer looking at me.

I would have killed for another touch. *Gladly*. I would have presented her with my crown if she'd asked for it. The only thing stronger than her hold on me in those few wild moments is the fear of losing myself.

At least she doesn't know her power.

Yet.

I'm used to the silent presence of my guards, three to five yards away, generally at the doors. Though I can enjoy their company off duty, we've settled into a rhythm where they don't interfere with my day in any way while shadowing me. My life would be far less agreeable if I were forced to consider their opinion at every turn.

Now I do turn to Koll. "What the ever-loving fuck was that?"

The knight exchanges a glance with his partner, Varen, and both shrug under their heavy armor, as clueless as me.

CHAPTER THIRTY
GIVE AND TAKE

I spend the entire ride glaring at the man in front of me in the bucket seat, wishing I could just leap out and strangle him.

The only thing holding me back is the fact that I'd be hanged for treason if I did. Or maybe beheaded. As both a noble and a freaking whore to the king, I might merit the courtesy of a swift execution.

I can't believe he kissed me. I can't believe I let him. And I sure as all seven hells would like to understand how I could have liked it. He had his hands all over me and my treacherous body dared to want more.

Then he made it all worse by calling me out on it.

After I set off in the wrong direction, running away from him more than toward something, he sent a guard after me, and the bulky coldblood was kind enough to escort me back to my room. Nissa and Lupa help me shed the stupid dress—or does it qualify as a piece of jewelry?

I expected to have to put yesterday's clothes, but

the king had several outfits brought to my room, and to my surprised, some were even tolerable. I found black slacks and paired them with a cropped green top under a blazer. I quite like the look, though I wouldn't have imagined it myself.

I only had time to dress before I was informed that we were heading back to Magnapolis.

Finally.

Except I am traveling with Zale, in a hovercraft smaller than the duke's, though the interior is more luxurious.

Objectively, I know the ride back to the city is much faster than the travel in my stepfather's cumbersome craft on the way in. Regardless of the actual speed of the vehicle, the journey feels like it lasts for days on end, with that infuriating kiss replaying at the back of my mind every second, and the fact that Zale's seated directly opposite me.

The king spends the entire ride paging through the alchemy manual I read before my first class, and I can tell he's not paying attention to a single word.

We've reached the mainland by the time I give in, breaking the intolerable silence. "Why do you even study alchemy? You can use magik!"

His icy eyes don't leave the page. "Why do you?"

I should have expected him to avoid a straight answer.

"It goes both ways, dearie. If you'd like knowledge about me to use as a weapon or a shield, you'll have to share your own weaknesses."

I huff. "It was a simple question."

Only nothing could ever be simple between Zale Devar and me. At least, not after that kiss.

He was, and is, my enemy. That much hasn't changed. From the get-go, he decided to play that part. But though I'm certain he still wants me gone and I'd love nothing more than to thrust my pretty dagger between his shoulder blades, I'd also wager he'd kiss me again before sending me on my way, and I wouldn't mind feeling the rough pressure of his lips before stabbing him to death. He's ruined a perfectly good enmity, muddling it in shades of desire and confusion.

"I have an innate ability with an element validated by the faculty, as well as a master's in spell crafting and summoning."

I'd like to say he's boasting, but he sounds matter-of-fact, almost bored.

"To qualify as a Master of the Eldritch Arts, one must be proficient in *all* forms of magiks, not just sorcery, or summoning, or elemental." He shuts the book and finally drags his icy gaze to mine. "I have no inclination to take metamorphosis, and alchemy was the closest equivalent."

I have a thousand more questions now.

He wants to be a Master of the Eldritch Arts. But why? He is the king of Ravelyn, with more power at his fingertips than most could dream of. Why seek another title?

And yet I suspect in his shoes I'd be the same, striving to learn everything I can, earn as many qualifications as possible.

I understand my own hunger for more, as I once

had very little. It makes less sense in his case.

"Your turn. Why alchemy, and not politics, or sciences, or literature?"

I look out the window, breaking eye contact first. He's answered my question, so I ought to be fair and return the favor, but I'm embarrassed. "Well, I can't do magiks, can I?"

"Can't you?" he questions pointedly. "I mean, have you ever attempted to?"

That makes little sense. "Core magiks are innate, right? Shifters turn in their puberty; witches start to release light or shade energy unbidden until they learn what to do with it. People know if they have magiks. I don't."

He leans forward and reaches for my hands, too fast for me to think of withdrawing.

"What are you doing?"

Zale's seeking my eyes, a frown between his delicate brows. I can tell he's calling to some energy by the mist of silver and green flashing in his eyes, and the delicious waves suddenly coursing through me, cloaking me in a comfortable, lulling embrace.

"Take it in, don't reject it."

I couldn't if I wanted to. I feel lighter than ever, the weights and worries on my shoulders shoved aside as the power whispers to me.

"Now direct it. Move it in your mind. It's yours to command as you please."

I try. By all the gods, I attempt to, but though the waves of magik adhere to me like they're meant for me, nothing stirs, at least not at my bidding.

I withdraw my hands, and return my attention to the window.

"Fascinating," Zale murmurs, speaking to himself as he leans back again.

"What?" I snap.

He considers his words carefully before settling on, "Any mage may share their energy willingly, and the youngest toddler will instinctively manipulate it, if they can wield magiks. You didn't."

I knew I couldn't, but my heart sinks all the same. My jaw tightens in annoyance. "I told you, I'm common."

"Mayhaps." Zale is visibly unconvinced. "Though the shade ought to have bypassed you entirely and aimed for my guards in the next compartment or been released in the wind. You sucked it in like a magnet, Helyn."

I can count on one hand the number of times he's used my name rather than a ridiculous nickname.

"So?"

The craft slowly lowers to the ground. I'm surprised we're already back to the city.

Instead of landing around Five, it moves to park before a white manor surrounded by a canal and a precisely manicured lawn of blue-green grass, bright despite the blinding summer heat. There's no water shortage this side of the city.

"Why aren't we returning to Five?"

"Because it's early afternoon on Grapurday," he replies like it makes sense. "Weekends last three days, not one, you know."

My jaw tightens. "I study on weekends. I have to go back to the library."

The truth is, I don't technically have to. I've read the materials for my next tests, and I'm running about three weeks ahead on all my assignments. But that doesn't mean I want to spend more time with Zale, especially now.

His company should be disagreeable as ever, but he withdrew his claws, not whispering a single insult the entire journey. I don't know what to make of any of this.

"The city will have heard of your appointment by now. You're going to be surrounded at every turn, questioned, and if the envious manage to, cursed. Five's not safe for you now. Not while you're alone."

"And whose fault is that?" I snap.

He doesn't seem the least bit ashamed. "Mine. Which is why you'll stay here."

I purse my lips, opening my own door before one of his servants get the chance. "I'll pass, thank you."

I'm surprised and grateful his house isn't fenced. It means I can burst out of there without having to beg to be let out like a dog.

I half expect one of his stern guards to catch up with me and drag me inside as I take off toward the avenue, but I am left alone.

"You know where to come when you change your mind."

I huff, grumbling curses about arrogant jerks on my way out.

CHAPTER THIRTY-ONE

THE PRIVATE CIRCLE

"Follow her," I order Koll. "From a distance, and discreetly. Only interfere if she's in danger."

He inclines his head, activating the communication device fitted at the base of his ear with a tap of his finger. "Replacement needed at the king's side, effective immediately, location Royal Lane, copy."

Koll waits for Helyn to reach the main avenue, her gait swift and her stance clearly annoyed. I find some solace in the fact that I'm getting under her skin faster than she gets under mine. Then when she reaches the corner, the captain of my guard trails after her.

I need to set up a permanent team of guards for her. And have rooms set up here. She won't last three days back at the dorm after the word get out that she's become first lady of Ravelyn.

I'm on my way to the front of the house when a familiar cry resounds in the clouded sky. I hear Talon before he circles overhead and soars down to my arm.

The black raven lifts his beak for a scratch and coos happily when I comply. "You have a message for me?" I ask him.

He mercilessly bites my finger, showing his discontent. I snort, and keep scratching him. Needy little thing. Only after the royal pet is fussed over to his liking does he allow me to take the parchment tied to his leg.

He sets off in the air as I read the short note.

I sigh. I could have brought Helyn back to Five, after all. "Change of plan," I tell Varen. "I'm wanted back at Five."

We're but a few short streets away from Five, and I still make my driver drop me off. The temperature is slightly cooler than it had been when I left yesterday, but the air is thick with moisture. It must have rained. The only thing I hate more than a warm summer day is a warm, humid summer day.

Five minutes later, I'm strolling inside the dorm, making straight for my apartment on the first floor.

"Should I be concerned that you're calling a meeting in *my* dorm, Reiks?" I ask, ignoring the other three students carelessly lounging on my furniture.

I know he's the one who called the meeting, and selected its location.

The giant-blooded prince smirks. "I didn't want to leave the dorms yet, and my room was occupied until now."

I'll bet.

I join him next to the window overlooking the courtyard between the dorms and the main building, and watch the tall, slender figure retreat as fast as her feet can carry her. "Ah, the future queen of Anderkan." I chuckle. So he's finally managed to catch his prey. "Is she aware of the fact that she's replaced dear Blythe yet?"

"Kinda," Reiks replies, amused. "She thinks it's temporary."

Unlike me, my old friend likes games and the thrill of the chase. Admittedly, underplaying his interest in Alis Frejr might be the smarter course of action. The girl doesn't like to make waves. "She'll figure it out at the wedding, with a bit of luck."

Natheran Reiks always gets what he wants. He makes sure of it, manipulating everyone with ease until they're exactly where he wants them. At his mercy.

The poor Frejr never had a chance.

"How about *your* future queen?" Now, Reiks smirks at me. "Still in denial?"

The fact that I know exactly to whom he's referring is alarming. "Don't be ridiculous. She's *common*."

I contacted Reiks for his opinion on whether a common ought to have Helyn's abilities. Anderkan has rejected magiks for centuries and though his blood is as full of power as mine, Reiks knows more than I do about their kind.

He told me nothing that I wouldn't have guessed myself. Commons are individuals, and no two are typically alike. Yes, it's entirely unusual for one of them to best one of us in any discipline, but there are plenty of dumb, weak demis, while others rise above the masses. The same can be said for their kind.

I'm not one to pretend false modesty; I know I am one of the strongest things in this part of the world, and I'm certainly not of average intellect. It *shouldn't* be possible for a common girl to best *me*.

Talking it out with Reiks won't shed any light on the matter, so I decide a change of subject is in order. "How is Blythe, by the way? Recovering well?"

Blythe Ostra, Reiks's former fiancée, used to be part of our little get-togethers before she faked her death to get out of marrying him, thereby also rejecting a crown and a life of luxury.

"Still designing clothes," he tells me. "Flaur agrees with her. There's even talk of a girl she's gone out with more than a couple of times."

I smile, glad for our old friend.

"Sometimes I envy her," Rovan Briar interjects from the settee, though I thought him focused on his conversation with the second princess of Vanemir and the first prince of Dorath.

"Alis?" Reiks asks, his mind clearly focused on his lover.

The Flauran prince snorts. "Not everyone wants to blow your dick, Nath. *Blythe*. I envy her. She got out. No more political circus for her. No more attempts on her life based on who she is, what she could become. She's free."

Reiks grimaces, the concept of freedom eluding him, unsurprisingly.

I understand why Rovan feels that way. His twin will wear the crown after their vapid mother croaks, but he's expected to act like a royal, reaping all of the duty and none of the benefits.

"Well, we aren't," Selina Aevar says. She's also a second-born, but unlike Rovan, she's been given no reason to resent her position. She and her elder sister get along. "So, we have to take care of this before it blows up in our faces."

She gestures to the coffee table in front of her, and I leave Reiks's side to look at it, frowning. "Is that from the rebels?"

A map of Xhera has been laid out, and I note that every capital was circled in bold pen. Magnapolis is crossed in red, but my attention stays on the circle over the Dark Keep.

Selina nods and I consider it again.

None of this makes sense. At first glance, I would have taken this for a plan of attack, missing tons of information, but with obvious targets. But who could hope to take *my* city, and to what purpose? The kingdom is ruled from the Whyte Fort these days.

"We need to make copies," Reiks decrees. "And call for council sessions in our respective kingdoms, and here in Magna."

It is the first relevant information we've managed to ferret out, and we need a lot more.

I can't say I'm as invested as the rest of my companions. For years now, an alliance of dissatisfied commons has taken to attacking nobles and demis, targeting us in various ways in order to seize the control of the world. Mostly they fail, but they're a nuisance all the same. There have been a few attempts at disruption by rebels in Ravelyn, but not as much as on the mainland, no doubt because our number of commons is far lesser.

I turn to the Dorathian prince, assuming that this piece of intelligence came from him. "Get your spy to keep digging."

I could have attempted to phrase my order like a request, but Aeron's mere presence irritates me.

There are few on Xhera whose company I relish and one of them was his half-brother. Now our friend Loken's disappeared after wild accusations for crimes he'd never commit—not without cause—and this smarmy git is next in line to sit on the throne of Dorath.

Not that in matters. That throne is nothing more than a seat. The true power of their country lies elsewhere, as I've learned every time my kingdom has needed anything from Dorath. Business is to be discussed with the merchant's guild, and everything else happens at the pleasure of the Wicked in charge of the assassin's guild. I don't need to force myself to treat that boy like an equal.

Reiks sends me an amused look, in clear agreement, before concluding the meeting with a terse, "I'll send Talon out. Call him if you have more."

Everyone else leaves, but these are my rooms, so I linger until I'm alone with the massive Anderkanian.

"You look like shit," he tells me.

I chuckle. I've barely slept, and I can count on him to call me out on it. "Still hotter than you."

The picture of confidence, Reiks leans back

against the wall, chin up. In many ways, we're opposites, he and I: his dark curls to my white-blond hair, a warm tan to my constant pallor, and a considerable bulk to my lithe figure. His cold eyes are grey, and mine a bright ocean blue. Rare are those who'd guess our mothers were sisters, both concubines to cold kings. I like to keep it that way. Someone tried to ensure I had no family left once. I won't make it easy for anyone to track down those of my blood again.

"What can I do for you?" he asks, always delighted to offer favors, collecting them like trophies.

He knows he could ask me whatever he wishes without my owing him anything, but men like Reiks are incapable of ceasing their machinations.

"I need to get in touch with Valina Frejr—her, specifically, not her sons, or daughters, or whatever other shields she likes to place between herself and the world."

The fact that I can't gain direct access to the witch although I am king grates, but there's nothing I can do about it. Valina rules a remote land surrounded by elder magiks, and heads the most powerful clan on the mortal kingdoms. She may not wear a crown, but she might as well. If she doesn't want to be disturbed, there's nothing the rest of us can do.

Reiks snorts. "Oh, is that all? Would you also like the keys to the eternal realm and the heart of a dragon?"

I shrug. "You managed to talk to her."

"Well, she wanted to talk to me." He scratches his chin. "How about calling for the international council?

We need to spread the word about the map, and she almost always attends it."

The idea has merit, though it places me in a position I don't care to occupy.

I'd have to take a stand on this silly rebellion that barely affects me.

Which means Reiks has placed me exactly where he wants me on the board.

I don't have much of a choice, though. If I want to ask Valina what she was doing in Ravelyn the day my family was slaughtered—and what she might have seen —I need to either go to her or make her travel here.

Only one of those options isn't suicidal.

"Sometimes, I hate you, cousin."

His shoulders shake with laughter. "Only because I'm smarter than you, Zale."

CHAPTER THIRTY-TWO
A DOSE OF REALITY

I park the speeder I picked up where I left it in the duke's courtyard in the same spot I used the last time I went to the undercity, right across the canal, before aiming straight for Glitter Lane.

I intended to ask after my crew after thanking Johel for the clothes she had delivered to me. Turns out, I don't need to. I approach stealthily, hiding behind a large lady, then a baker pulling a cart offering cream puffs. Sticking a coin in his hand, I grab one of the pastries and stuff it in my mouth, right before leaping out of his shadow and grabbing Alva by the shoulders.

"Ha!" I scream.

She yells and throws a punch while twirling on her feet with the agility of a cat. Expecting the blow, I block it and grin at my old friend.

"Hel!" she screeches and envelops me in a bear hug. "What in the seven hells!"

Khel grins from Johel's side, biting into a green apple. "Hey, kid. Long time."

I wave at him as best I can behind Alva's back. "Kid? I'm still your boss."

He huffs out a derisive snort, and Alva finally lets go.

"Yeah, about that." She smacks her lips. "You know, we were just saying, it's awesome you give tons of money to really help the neighborhood, and we're *so* glad you get to study uptown. It's one in a million. Exactly what we wanted for you."

She shoots Khel a look, desperate for support. He takes another bite of his apple, leaving her to it, like the dick he is.

"But, well, Hel..."

"You figure an undercity crew leader ought to live in the undercity," I finish for her, taking pity. It's not like the idea hasn't crossed my mind before.

To be frank, I'm relieved she brought it up. I would have felt awkward as hell, letting them know I plan to leave the crew.

I'm a student, and after I learn everything I can, to know just how I can make a difference in the world, to truly change things for our kind structurally from the bottom up? I'll be something else. A crew leader isn't one of them.

I didn't realize it when I first took the duke's offer to let me attend Five, but I do now. I'll never live in the undercity again. Anyone born here has one single focus: leaving. It's not my home, so much as the streets that forged me.

I love so many people in the lanes surrounding Glitter Lane, and this neighborhood, this village, is the only family I've ever had, yet while I can't see where I'll go in the future, I know it won't be here.

I am Neleda's daughter, after all. Unlike her, I don't intend to abandon anyone, ever.

"When should we have a race to choose the next leader?" I ask Alva, smiling.

"You don't mind?"

"Why would I? Crew races are the best parties." I only pretend to misunderstand her to show her how planning my replacement is a non-issue. "Tell me how things have been."

"Hot as purgatory. I can't wait for autumn," Khel grumbles.

"Well, consider yourself lucky. I just came back from Ravelyn, and it's a miracle I still have ten toes."

They make me spill every detail I can remember, Johel demanding to know about the outfits, Khel curious about the architecture, and Alva, everything else. I don't say a word about my pearl dress, but other than that, I don't conceal a thing and their questions leave no stone unturned.

I consider not bothering to share the news of my new title, but they're likely to hear it through the grapevine. Better it comes from me.

"He named you his freaking concubine?" Alva gasps. "Against your will? Get out of my way. I'll skin that dick alive!"

I don't doubt she'd try, either. "He's not forcing me to do anything, don't worry." I shrug. "He's just a bully, trying to teach me a lesson. I'm not letting him get to me." Not much, in any case. To Johel, I say, "The green dress helped a lot."

Her grin shows off the gap in her front teeth. "That's my girl."

Alva keeps grumbling about puny kings and their tiny little peckers, and Khel's mouth flattens into a thin line. "How many concubines does he have?"

"None. Well, just me."

"Hm. And you say he doesn't force himself on you?"

I can't help thinking back to that all-consuming, domineering kiss. Zale might have crossed many lines, but I can hardly call myself an unwilling participant. If it had been up to me, I would have kept him right there, wrecking havoc in my core while setting my body on fire forever.

"He doesn't. And if he dared, I have a brand-new blade to pierce him with."

My friend snorts. "Like you'd take a demi."

I take the opportunity to recount how I did just that, though Adelaid Gyrth isn't in the same ball park as Zale Devar.

It's well past dusk when I finally head back to my speeder after catching up with the crew and some of the neighborhood. I'm stuffed full of street food and weak ale, and sweltering in the heat, even more oppressive now after I spent a day in the winter.

This time, my craft isn't here. I sigh, hardly surprised. I would have stolen it given half a chance, too.

I walk back to Five, exhausted by the hour-long trek

in the heat. Dragging my feet to the third floor, I only lift my gaze to my door when I'm mere feet away from it.

That's when I see the eager crowd planted in front of it, awaiting my return.

"There she is! That's Helyn!"

"Is it true the king proposed in front of the entire white court?"

"Who designed the pearl dress, Helyn?"

"Were you truly not wearing anything underneath?"

By all seven hells! I'm going to strangle Zale.

Just after I ask him to let me stay in his place.

I turn on my heels so fast, escaping the crowd by shouting irrelevant excuses until I'm back at the gate. Then, naturally, warm heavy rain starts, drenching me to the bone. By the time I'm back in front of the imposing manor I stormed away from just hours ago, I no doubt look like a drowned rat.

I'm surprised the king opens his door himself, given that he must have hundreds, if not thousands of servants at his command.

"Not a word," I hiss.

He presses his lips together, but doesn't even attempt to stop his smirking.

Zale isn't capable of remaining silent for long. "I'll have your maid draw you a bath. Dinner's in an hour. Nothing formal."

He steps aside to let me in.

CHAPTER THIRTY-THREE
ADAMANTLY MORTAL

H aving a woman in my household isn't as uncomfortable or distracting as I assumed it would be, perhaps because it is Helyn and she doesn't make a habit of demanding much of me.

All she wanted was access to the library. I've barely seen her since.

I know for a fact the servants I brought back from Ravelyn for her benefit—two maids she seemed to like —informed her of breakfast and lunch, but by dinner, she hasn't seen fit to leave the company of my books.

I don't usually have the private dining room set up, preferring simple dinners at my desk when I'm alone, but I had the table dressed there all weekend, and dined with no one other than the eight footmen in attendance.

By dinner on Fevaday night, I've had enough. I stalk to the library doors and knock three times, before remembering this is my house. I push the doors open.

I'm unprepared for the picture waiting for me.

Helyn has dragged a fur rug to a burning oversized fireplace that's never been lit in the fifteen years of my occupancy. She lies on the floor at the hearth, cocooned in two thick blankets she must have taken from her bed and surrounded by a dozen books. Her head's propped up on top of two large leather volumes, and she reads, eyes half closed.

"What in the seven hells are you doing?"

"Zale." She sits up, hooded eyes unfocused as she looks up to me.

"Didn't your ladies tell you it was dinnertime?" I frown.

"They did. Don't trouble yourself on my account, I had some soup brought up earlier..." She frowns, as though trying to remember how much earlier.

By the heavens, this woman shouldn't be trusted to take care of her basic needs. "You need to eat. And sleep on a bed, not on the hard floor!"

She waves a dismissive hand. "My room is freezing. And you have the most fascinating collection. I've never heard of half of the books here—private, limited editions, handwritten accounts."

"Why didn't you tell your maids you'd like to have a fire lit in your room?"

She grimaces. "Why inconvenience them? I'm perfectly comfortable here."

I blow out a slow breath. "Helyn, you're the stepdaughter of a duke and the first lady of Ravelyn. If you're cold, you say so. Understood?"

"You're unnecessarily bossy. But I like your library."

It's only when she chuckles that I think to check her temperature.

I move to her side and press my hand to her forehead. She's always warm to me, but the burning skin, and the fact that she let me examine her without a word of protest, settles matters. "You're running a fever."

"I'm fine," she scoffs.

I sigh, bend to her and take her by the knees and back. I lift her and carry her out of the room, calling, "I need a healer." There always are eyes and ears listening around me, discreet as they might make themselves. "And send someone to light a fire."

The closest footman rushes through the halls. "Where, my lord?"

I consider the question. "Everywhere. At least one per floor, and all of the fireplaces in Helyn's quarters."

It never occurred to me that the temperature I keep my house at through the year by ways of spells would be harmful to her, though it should have. She's no coldblood. She's no demi at all. This state she's in proves it like nothing else could. Variances in temperatures might make one of us more or less comfortable, but the weather can't make us sick.

"Why are you making such a fuss?" she moans.

I lower her to her bed, brushing a strand of copper curls off her wet forehead. "Because you look like death, Helyn, that's why."

"Hel," she replies. At first, I think she's cursing, but she adds, "Everyone calls me Hel."

"Hel."

No insult or praise I could have come up with suits her better.

The two coldblood maids are still building a fire up when Koll comes in, escorting a witch.

"She needs to be seen right away." I don't like the rising panic in my chest.

The tanned lady in a light sundress comes closer, and sits close by.

She checks her temperature and smiles at me. "Nothing alarming."

I didn't realize how tense I was until I finally exhale.

"Have you eaten today, sweet pea?" the witch asks Helyn—Hel.

She frowns. "I wasn't too hungry. Nissa brought me soup, I think."

The servant looks up from the fire. "Yes, for lunch, at your request, my lady. You didn't eat much of it. Or the porridge at breakfast."

I explode. "Why wasn't I made aware of this?"

Both maids jump.

"Sir, she ate well yesterday," Lupa whines apologetically.

I redirect my anger where it belongs, at the foolish girl shivering on her bed. "How did you survive so long if this is how you take care of yourself?"

She chuckles as though I've made a joke.

"She's fine," the witch repeats. "It's just a little cold. You were out in the rain yesterday, yes?"

"A little," she admits.

I remember laughing at her drenched clothes and

the wet curls plastered to her skin. In hindsight, the scene is far less amusing.

"She was in Ravelyn less than two days ago," I add. "The change of temperature can affect commons, right?"

The witch nods. "You'll have to be careful to stay warm and dry, little lady," she admonishes Hel, digging into her oversized leather bag.

She retrieves a fist-sized blue flask and hands it to me. "See that she drinks three healthy sips now, the same before bed and in the morning. She should be fine tomorrow."

"Thank you," I say, making her laugh.

"For the amount you're paying me, you don't have to thank me, Your Majesty."

She soon leaves, along with the maids I send to bring refreshments and fresh bedding back. I'm alone, standing next to her bed awkwardly.

She sits up slowly, the effort making her grunt, and extends her hand to me.

I take it, and Hel chuckles. "The medicine, silly."

"Right." Jaw tight, I hand her the potion, and watch her drink three times.

She scowls. "It tastes like feet."

"That's what you get for letting yourself get sick." I don't think I'm likely to forgive her for this brand of uncharacteristic stupidity.

I like my Helyn smart and feisty.

I drag the armchair from next to her handsome dressing table close to the bed and sit.

"Are you staying here?"

"Well, you're clearly incapable of keeping yourself alive, so I'll have to, won't I?"

The room soon grows uncomfortably warm, and the maids bring her a cover on top of it.

I remain there for the rest of the night.

CHAPTER THIRTY-FOUR
THE KING'S GUARD

I wake in the early morning, according to the light out of my window, with a slight headache and the acute need to jump into a pit, embarrassed beyond words.

I can't believe I let myself get sick here, in all places. The images assaulting my mind as I drag myself upward make me want to hide for the rest of my days. Did I honestly let Zale carry me in his arms like a bloody princess?

"My lady!" Lupa rushes to my side. "You're not to exert yourself at all today. King's orders."

I roll my eyes. "I'm not sure the king wants me to wet my bed."

She lets me go to the bathroom in peace, but she's waiting at the door when I come out.

"Breakfast will be up soon, Lady Helyn."

I sigh. "I'm fine. And I have to get back to Five."

Her mouth falls open. "Oh, but you're unwell."

"I've been worse, trust me." Returning to my

bedside table, I finish the dregs of the witch's portion. Gosh, the mushroom-and-fart combination is disgusting. "See? I'm all better."

"But the king—"

"I'll see the king on my way out," I assure her.

I open my door, and come face-to-face with Zale, who glowers like the very sight of me offends his sensibilities.

"You should be in bed."

"You paid a witch to ensure I'd recover in record time. Thanks for that by the way," I think to add.

His hand moves to my forehead, palm down.

"I'm not a child," I grumble.

"Then don't act like one." His terse tone might have annoyed me less if yesterday's events hadn't proved him right.

I should have eaten, drunk more, and paid attention when my head began not feeling right, but his collection of books was engrossing. I figured I was just getting tired.

"You're much cooler," he allows. "If you want to return to the university, I'll take you, but you will return home if you're feeling unwell, yes?"

Home. What a strange word for a house I've slept in one feverish night—a house that belongs to him.

"Sadly, I don't think I have one of those."

Where is my home, exactly? The crowded dorm, the redbrick ducal house in the next avenue, this huge manor I've barely explored?

None of the above. But it makes sense to come back here, for now.

"I have a council meeting tonight. Don't forget to have dinner, yes?"

"In the Hall of Peace?" I ask. The international council is where all the decisions about the mortal realms of Xhera take place.

It makes sense that Zale has a seat on it. I'm yet again witnessing the difference of power between he and I.

"I'd love to see it."

He cocks a brow, surprised. "Truly? They're endless, boring, and often pointless."

I nod, ready to remind him that thanks to the title he bestowed upon me, I have the right to accompany him wherever I please.

I don't need to. "All right. Bring a pillow and attempt not to drool."

At this time, everyone's either in a late class or heading to dinner. I'm sprinting through the empty, familiar corridors, when I hit an unexpected obstacle around a corner. I fall back on my ass and my library books scatter all around me.

Shit.

Some of those books are quite valuable. I hope I didn't damage the binding.

"Sorry!" The collision is definitely my fault. I've been on edge since I woke up—actually, since we finished that experiment—and my restless energy didn't allow for caution.

I look up to see the tallest woman I've ever laid eyes on. Eerily thin, with gorgeous, wide green eyes and silky brown hair, she belongs on the cover of a magazine. Adelaid Gyrth would look like a pixie next to this statuesque beauty.

I expect her to be as rude and obnoxious as everyone else I've dealt with in this place, but she smiles at me and bends to help me pick the dusty volumes. "No worries." Piling the last book on top of the one I just stacked, she tilts her chin to my books. "You're okay with all those?"

"Hm?" I'm too unfocused to immediately understand, then her words replay in my mind. "Oh, I'm fine. I just need to bring them back to the library, and I hate making too many trips," I ramble nervously. "I'm sorry I didn't see you. You're sure you're not hurt?"

"Not even a little. Do you need help?" she offers openly, stunning me.

There are some good people here after all. Maybe she's a common like me, though I doubt it. She holds herself like a queen. I can't quite pinpoint how or why, but I'd swear I'm in the presence of someone important, consequential.

I decide I don't need to find out. No matter my first impression of her, I've had more than my fair share of brushes with nobility for a while. "I'm good, thanks."

I race to the library and pick up the books I need for my next three. To my horror, I find it as crowded as my bedroom was, with brazen strangers happy to ply me with ridiculous and highly personal questions.

I bolt, and consider returning to my dorm. As it is likely I'll find it equally under siege, I drag the books all the way back to Zale's, grumbling about missing my baby blue speeder all the way.

I've only just left the campus when a tall coldblood dressed in black catches up with me. I recognize him, I think, though I can't pinpoint where from.

"With your leave, I'll assist you, Lady Helyn."

I blink up at him. "I'm fine, thank you."

"Pardon me, my lady, but that's a lot of books," he says, eyeing my pile. "And we are going the same way."

"How would you know where I'm going?" I say, eyes narrowing.

He winces and scratches his head. "There's no nice way of putting it. I've been following you." Seeing my expression, he rushes to add, "On the king's orders. I'm one of your guards—that is, until a permanent retinue of knights are assigned to you."

I'm not sure I believe him at first, but I focus on his eyes and find that I do recognize them. Usually, they're the only thing I see, as he typically wears a silver helmet with full armor.

"I see. Well, in that case..." I hand him three of the seven volumes in my arms.

He snorts and takes two more.

We chat on the short walk to Zale's. His name is Koll and he's from the southern isle—though not my stepfather's holdings. He asks about the undercity, and I tell him all about my grandmother.

When we reach the manor, he escorts me to the library—and a good thing too, as I forgot the way—and takes a seat on the opposite side of the study table that's been brought close to the fire since yesterday.

I suppose the king didn't like my using his rug as a desk.

Koll's company isn't unpleasant, and he does order lunch, and then a snack around four, no doubt under the king's command.

I can't help but wonder that I am now under the protection of the king who despised me and did his best to crush me with shame just a few days ago.

And worse yet: I let him take care of me, indirectly or not.

CHAPTER THIRTY-FIVE
VOICELESS

I've seldom come as far uptown as the main city square, and by the time Zale's hovercraft lands in front of it, I'm as excited as a little girl.

The square is packed with city folk, food stands, dancers and magicians sharing their skills for a few coins.

I could spend hours just walking around the square, but we've arrived just before the start of the council session, and Zale leads us straight inside the fifty-foot tall amphitheater where the lords of the world decide our fates.

"You'll take my family's box, and you won't cast a vote tonight. If you wish for a voice, you'll need to ask your stepfather to name you at the council." Zale's long strides don't wait for me. "Or ask me," he adds, shooting me a quick glance over his shoulder.

Right. Like I'm about to beg him for a favor.

Two days ago, Zale acted like my enemy and I responded in kind. Yesterday, he took care of me, and I don't quite know what to do with that—or with the kind guard he's assigned to me.

My asking for something is a step I'm not about to take. I don't know where this strange dynamic of ours is leading. Following the flow is easier.

The large box holds half a dozen seats, and I take the one closest to the edge, to have a better view.

Thousands of such boxes surround the sand floor of the arena in the middle, and most are occupied. I don't recognize most of the long, severe faces in formalwear, but most seem young—though with demi, I never know.

We've arrived late, and the council session starts only moments after Zale strides through the arena to reach the elevated platform at its center. I note the presence of Salvar Rhodes by his side, though he doesn't notice me, too preoccupied by whispering in the ear of the king.

The ecclesiastic figure in fine white raiment stands. "We've gathered today to address the threat organized rebels might pose to our respective countries, and to Xhera as a whole," he calls, his voice rough and aged.

Unlike most around the oval table set on the main platform, the holy man's old, and thoroughly common.

I've seldom seen a rich common man, and I find that I don't like the sight. His protuberant belly and red nose speak of a life of excesses. No amount of makeup or fine clothing can hide it. At least, the demis remain beautiful despite their many sins. This man looks like the worst of us.

He continues. "For years, we've been at peace. A precarious, uneasy peace, as each kingdom retains customs that may offend their neighbors. But peace nonetheless. I, who have seen the last war, see the value in peace. With this in mind, I propose we hear these rebels. Listen to their demands, and reasonably give a voice to the changes our younger generations want to see."

A beautiful woman clad in black—with a deep tan and striking eyes shining red even at this distance—snorts. "You'll remember your order started the last war because you wanted change then, too. You wanted a world where I, and those like me, don't exist, so that the commons might feel more relevant. How did that go for you?" She speaks with saccharine hatred.

The old man's eyes never meet hers. "We're not rehashing the old days. Who knows what these young men and women demand this time?"

"If I were to hazard a guess?" Zale says. My stepfather tries to speak in his ear, but Zale waves him aside without a care. "More money, mostly. That seems to be the kind of shit people want."

I grin. He's got that right.

A delicate, beautiful lady smiles, though it never reaches her amber eyes. "We have been working on improving life as a whole. It's been slow progress, like any real change, but look at what we have achieved in the last hundred years. I remember a time when half the kingdoms didn't have any running water or electricity."

I don't know who she is, but I decide I hate her.

We're supposed to be content with the scraps off her table?

"Commons don't see that, because they don't live a hundred years," a brown-skinned man says, arrogant and dismissive. "It's all about the now with them."

My teeth grind. What in the seven hells is this? And why isn't Zale saying a thing? Surely he knows better.

We're not indulgent or ungrateful, or whatever else they imply. We're condemned to remain at the bottom because no job pays a decent wage unless it requires magiks.

The woman in black grunts. "Tell me you didn't call for a meeting to talk in circles again. Some of us have things better to do."

"I didn't call for this meeting at all." The holy man holds his head high. "The young king has something to share."

I watch Zale stand, and wonder if he's about to tell these idiots they're mistaken.

Then I remember who he is.

Why would he come to our defense when he thinks exactly like the others?

I shouldn't have come here.

"Our intelligence retrieved this map from a rebel compound right after a meeting." The hologram of a large map of the continent appears in the space above their platform, and though focusing on it hurts my head, I do look.

"It is our belief," Zale says, his voice toneless, "that they mean to attack all relevant cities in one strike. I'd like to call a vote. We need to call martial law, increase the protection of each one of our courts, and lend forces to the peace warriors of Magnapolis in order to prepare."

My jaw drops. I can't believe what I'm hearing.

Seriously? We're at the brink of a war and he didn't even think to tell me?

"An attack of that magnitude is improbable," a beauty in deep purple says. "Our castles are well guarded, often by demis. The rebels must realize that would be suicide."

The delicate woman so inclined to criticize my kind sneers. "And yet they've brazenly struck blow after blow at us the last few years. They might dare start a civil war throughout Xhera. We'll crush them, though."

"Will you? Don't get me wrong, you might end up victorious in the long term. But if every common rebel of Xhera were to focus on six points all at once, and you're unprepared?" The woman in black seems amused. "I'd say heads are going to roll. Not that it has anything to do with us. I don't see the Darklands targeted."

I surmise who she is now. Valina Frejr, the leader of the Darklands, and head of the greatest clan of witches in Xhera. No wonder she's unruffled.

Zale doesn't seem impressed by her. "If we fall, who do you suggest might be the target of the new regime?"

"I can handle common soldiers," the witch replies.

No one respects my kind at all here, and we don't have a single voice.

A young man, crowned and serene, who until then

was silent, smiles pleasantly at her. "The might of five countries against you? I'd pay to see you fall."

"You already did. Twice. I'm still here." Little as I like any of them, I have to admire the witch's confidence. "Let's vote, as the boy says. All those in favor for reinforcing the capitals and Magnapolis?"

Zale's hand shoots up, but no one else's joins his around the table.

Seeing movement around me, I look around, noticing that in the boxes around mine, some of the men and women are also taking part in the vote.

I remember what Zale told me earlier: I don't have a voice here.

Not yet.

I will next time. I'll see to it.

The holy man stands to announce, "Five hundred and thirty-three votes. The motion is dismissed."

- - -

The woman studying me with her unflinching stare looks much younger than me, and carries herself with the kind of nonchalant confidence I've only seen in people like us—those at the top of the food chain.

"What makes you think I remember a party some fifteen years ago?"

That's how she's going to play it? "I don't know... maybe because there was a massacre in the middle of the night after you left."

"That's fair," Valina Frejr admits. "Well, your father

wanted my help, and he kept bothering my sons and daughters, so I went to tell him in no uncertain terms that I wasn't interested. I didn't remain long, and saw almost no one."

I sigh, frustrated. She could be lying, but I doubt it. She has too much power to bother with subterfuge. "What did he want from you?"

"Protection." She has the decency to make a face. "Clearly, he needed it. I'm sorry for what happened to your family, Devar. You children didn't deserve it."

I note how she talks of my siblings and me, but doesn't say a word of my predecessor. "What did he need protection from?"

"He didn't say," she states. "And if you want my advice, I wouldn't waste my energy on revenge. I'm sure nostalgia has colored your perception, but your father was..."

"Cruel, cold, and selfish," I finish for her. "What of my sister, the other children? What of my mother, and the women whose only sin was ambition?"

The witch sighs. "He didn't say," she repeats. "But I know many threats were made against him because of his decision to reestablish indentured service."

That's the first I hear of that. "We've not had indentures for centuries."

"And had your father had his way, you wouldn't be saying that now. The motion was buried with him. See, retaining control of both of the islands, and pleasing himself as well as all his women was growing expensive. Claiming slaves in all but name for the debts of their families seemed like a good way to replenish the royal coffers, I suppose. That's the last in a long list of egocentric decisions that marked his rule."

Seven hells, he was even more of a tool than I remember. "I understand why someone got rid of him. But the entire family?"

Valina's smile seems a little sad. "When was the last time you made a decision for any reason but your entertainment, little Devar?"

I narrow my eyes. What does she know about me, to throw accusations of this sort?

"You're cruel. It is in your nature. Those you love best, you'll tease and trick for fun. The blood of the fae does not wane with time, especially mixed with that of an immortal. It is not natural for your kind to rule over theirs, child."

"You're saying you think me unfit to rule." The insult wouldn't needle so much if it wasn't tinged with a bit of truth.

"I'm saying you should have ruled a fairy court in the wild lands. For all the words they choose to describe themselves, demis, halfbloods, the inhabitants of the mortal kingdoms are just that. Mortals."

"Hypocritical, coming from you."

"I'm no queen," she snaps. "Those under my care, I protect. Do you?"

"So, what, you'd have me give up my crown?"

"I'd have you deserve it, child."

I decide I dislike this woman quite intensely, though her words aren't likely to leave me anytime soon. "Why not kill me then? If the traitors believed, like you, that the Devars aren't worthy of the throne."

"Isn't that obvious?"

I'm entirely clueless.

"My, it's a good thing you're pretty. I refused to come to a man's aid and a hundred corpses were burned high the next day, Devar."

My jaw ticks. She can't mean it. "You?"

Valina shrugs. "I let it be known that if the last child was taken, I'd look a little closer, is all."

And it's enough. The threat of Valina Frejr's fury has served as a shield I didn't know I had for most of my life.

I'm about to thank her, when the ground beneath my feet shakes and collapses.

CHAPTER THIRTY-SIX

THE FALL

T he session's over, and I'm still reeling.

I don't want to see Zale, or anyone, after hearing them spit on common folk for an entire hour, so I get out of there fast, eager to get to the square.

The crowd is still thick, celebrating leaders who don't care about them at all. Today was only about protecting their own interests.

I approach a food stand. "I'll have a meat bun, if you please."

"What lovely manner, miss."

I wince at seeing a common old man treat me like one of them.

I suppose in these fancy clothes of mine, I'm costumed into a lady.

I don't think I like the thought.

I overpay him with a gold instead of a copper and savor my bun as I wander around the square, stopping to watch every stand.

I smile at a magician hiding cards in his sleeve with the speed of a true sorcerer, when a thundering sound makes my heart drop to my stomach. I scream, along with the rest of the square. They scatter in every direction, panicked, the mob crushing this way and that.

I'm thrown along the tide of bodies, and push to my feet.

I roll to the side just in time to avoid a boot to my head, but take one in my stomach.

Grunting, I force myself to my feet again and rush to the only place that feels safe to me: the nearest wall. Wincing, my belly still sore, I leap to the closest window. Climbing with a stomach wound is never fun, but adrenaline is on my side. I make myself scale the smooth wall of the rich property, until I reach the roof.

***

I only have time to summon a wall of ice overhead before the hard white stone collapses.

I know it won't be enough, yet my thoughts, instead of remaining focused on my impending demise, are fixed on her.

Helyn is in the Hall of Peace. I brought her here. She's going to die because of me.

The entire ceiling falls and cracks against a black mist, dispersing before it hits me. Rather than taking time to thank the witch by my side, I close my eyes and direct every single bit of my focus through the spacious surroundings until my mind locks on her.

She's alive.

Alive and alone in a crazed stampede. I need to get out of here.

"Take the tunnel, I'll hold it," Valina tells me.

I finally think to offer the thanks I owe her for so many things, but her skin exudes a flash of golden light, and in next moment, she disappears.

By tunnel, she means the pile of crumbled stone. Her dark mist forms a cylindrical wall, barely the size of a man, and I run through it, not letting myself question what might happen if she's distracted and lets go.

When I emerge on the other side, I reach a mostly intact hall supported by three of its seven columns. Sprinting toward the closest exit I know of, my attention is so focused on Helyn, who climbs away from the square to safety, I don't even see the men in front of me before they call out.

"Hey, you! Stop where you are unless you want a laser through your brain, demi scum."

I skid to a stop mere inches away from the blaster he points right at my face.

I take in his appearance: heavy boots, brown, nondescript hunting clothes. He's plain, with a rich salt-and-pepper beard and almost no hair on his head.

He could be anyone of the billion average male commons on the continent right now. My first instinct is to freeze his veins but instead, I smile and tell him, "But you want to please me. Don't you?"

Many assume I need to call to some power to use

my influence. What they don't understand is that seducing away the will of others is what I am. I have to focus to prevent myself from doing it.

His eyes glaze over and he lowers the blaster. I snatch it from his hands and throw it aside. "Go to sleep."

Hopefully, he doesn't hit his head too hard on the marble floor where he crashes with a numb thud. After my effort to use nonlethal force, that'd be a waste.

I've almost made it to the south entrance when I encounter another obstacle—several common men, armed with the same type of fast laser weapon, point all of their weapons at me.

"That's the boy king!"

"Let's take him to command."

Command? They're that organized?

"Surrender or die, scum!" one of them demands.

Lasers are as fast as the speed of light, and one of them, aimed at the right spot, would be enough to kill me.

I might have spared the first man, but he posed no threat to me. This mob is another matter. There are two dozen of them, and should one strike true between my eyes, I'd be on the ground in seconds.

I'm but a few feet away from the main square, and I can still sense Helyn far too close. Should I make use of my best defense, there's no guarantee I wouldn't freeze her too. I can't risk it. Not even to save my neck.

And influencing one person or two at a time is one thing, but there's no way to do it to all of them at once.

Shit.

I hold my hands up in surrender, vowing to destroy every single one of them.

Just as soon as I get away and ensure Hel's safe, and far away from this city.

I didn't take Reiks seriously enough when he warned us that this rebellion was nigh. Now I'm paying the price.

From my perch, I watch in silent horror as the city explodes around me.

Left and right, the buildings detonate one after the next in a cloud of dust and fire.

I think about the map, and I know then what it was Zale strived to prevent.

He failed, but even if he had been successful, his effort would have come far too late.

I need to get back home. From here, with a clear view of the city, I can tell no one bothered to bombard the lanes. And no wonder. If the noble men were right, and this horror comes from commons, they aren't about to attack their own.

I don't know what makes me remain just where I am until I see them.

A dozen men, clapping and clamoring in victory as they encircle Zale, pushed forward at spearpoint with his hands bound.

It would be oh so easy to leave him to his fate. Let him reap the consequences of thousands of years of pain and indifference toward my kind. He's the cruel golden son of this broken world, this system that keeps people like me crushed within its talons. Objectively, he deserves this. Something savage inside me tells me to stay out of it. Just watch from a distance. I don't have to do anything at all. Just watch. Like the nobles watch while the plebes starve and suffer. I can finally be one of them. Maybe someone can get me popcorn.

Except I can't bear it.

My instincts tell another tale. In the last weeks, I've gotten to know Zale, and those like him—the demis ruling our world. I've dined with the monsters, feasting on the best cuts rather than the crumbs left over for the common blood. I've even struck up a strange and weak, uneasy friendship of sorts along the way—a day-old relationship wrapped in lies and unsaid truths, ready to be ripped apart at the slightest wind.

And I remember that kiss.

That disturbing kiss.

Beyond anything personal, I know what letting Zale die today by the hand of people like me will mean for tomorrow. The demis aren't on top because of their money, their many comforts, or the fact that their bellies are always full. The one percent rule over us because of power, simple as that. The abilities they were born with cannot be vanquished. Not when it takes a hundred of us to kill the least of them. The world would be painted red with common blood before we dethrone those who wield magic. We might have exiled the gods a thousand years ago, but the only reason why that endeavor worked was because we had their descendants on our side.

If Zale succumbs today, another one of *them* will take his throne tomorrow. My stepfather, if we're lucky. In all probability, someone far worse. I've seen his court. We'll be exchanging one monster for another. Likely, a worse option.

And as they say, better the devil you know... especially when said devil isn't as bad as I first believed.

I make my choice in an instant, leaving the relative, temporary safety of my rooftop to return to the ground.

I grab a discarded cloak from the floor, three times my size, and wrap it around me. Taking care to run in the same direction as the few confused, scared civilians dashing away from the square, I follow the procession leading Zale away from a distance. I'm one among a million, never worth a second look.

Finally, I reach an empty alley between a laundry and an alcohol store claiming to be open all day and night. It's closed now.

My muscles protest the exertion after so many months of leisure and comfort. I've grown weak.

I've been weak before. It didn't stop me from surviving then. It won't now.

I climb the smooth surface of the wall, hopping on top of the ale pint sign, then jumping atop the balcony on the second floor before the flimsy neon sign registers my weight.

When my feet hit the roof, I drop to a crouch and survey the burning city at my feet.

Funny. Weeks in high town, and I never felt at home. It looked too perfect from down below. Clean, polished, peaceful. Now, there are screams, heavy clouds of smoke, the stench of sweat and blood clog the air, and I finally recognize this city. The rich streets of Magnapolis, the golden capital, isn't much different from the undercity.

My brain kicks in, tying together the maps I glanced at so many moons ago and the layout I see before my eyes. We're perhaps six, seven hundred yards from Royal Lane, but heading there would be a mistake. I've no doubt the men holding the king will waste no time bringing him to their superiors—they're too far down in the pecking order to make a decision themselves. They would have taken the main streets— heavily guarded as they are, avoiding the thick of the battle wouldn't have crossed their mind.

Though my fancy, noble-made boots are hardly made for any type of exertion, I manage to keep my balance as I dart from rooftop to rooftop, scaling the city faster than I thought possible, and unnoticed. Even if anyone would think to look up, the smoke is too thick, and I, too used to moving undetected.

I find them faster than expected. Twelve men at his back, twelve at his front. One holds the tip of his bayonetted blaster to Zale's back, urging him forward.

My lips curl in distaste. A natural enough response to being anywhere near his highness for weeks, but now, my disgust is directed toward the foolish man holding his sharp weapon so close to Zale. Doesn't he realize that one false move, and he could impale a fucking king?

"If you can hear me, glance to your left right now," I whisper low.

I don't know much about his nature. Some demis have acute hearing, and I pray he figures among them.

I'm relieved to see him look to the closest house, casually. With a sigh, I continue, "There are two of your guards at the next intersection, poised to ambush your attackers. They're going to die," I tell him, matter-of-fact. "The rebels will be distracted for a few seconds— just a few seconds. I need you to jump into the canal. Nod if you understand."

I can tell he dislikes this plan, even from a distance, even without hearing a word. His sharp look around, to try to catch my gaze, is all I need.

"Fall in line or die. Those are your choices, Devar."

The company approaches the intersection. One step. Another one. A third.

I silently scale down the wall lounging the canal, until I land on one of the small boats docked along the jetty.

This is just another escape. I've survived hundreds, maybe thousands, of them. Except I was running from lane soldiers with magik, not fellow commons until now.

I can do this. I can do this.

I have to.

And so does he.

CHAPTER THIRTY-SEVEN

AT DAGGER'S POINT

I can't see a thing from my vantage point, but I can hear the commotion. It's now or never. Zale will have either followed my advice or opted to fight two dozen men out of stupid pride—or loyalty to his guards.

Three, two, one...

A sigh of relief crosses my lips when I hear the first man scream, "He's running! Catch him! The king!"

Zale leaps in the air, just as the boat I stole passes underneath him. He lands with a groan, wincing. "Hold on," I say, engaging the engine to speed up as fast as it can go.

Some of the common men run along the canal, others jump in the water, but they're no match for the speed of a boat.

My heart feels like it's beating at a thousand miles an hour when we lose them around a sharp corner.

They'll catch up eventually. It's now or never.

"Let's jump."

"What? We need to get to the sea, charter a boat to head north."

"How many thousands of men will wait for you at the harbor? For *me*," I amend.

They'll all speak about me, too, soon enough.

"Hel..."

I take my ridiculous, ruby-encrusted dagger from its sheath in my cloak and twirl it around my wrist, for no other reason than to let him understand just how well I can wield a blade, before bringing the tip to his chin.

Zale has the gall to chuckle. I want to punch him. Does he realize how close I am to stabbing him and counting my losses?

I'm so irritated at him after the council session, I perfectly understand the commons who wanted to bring it all down.

"Here's how it's going to work, Your Highness. First, you're going to listen to me, now. I'm smarter than you, and this is my city. Second, you're *never* going to mess with me again. Ever. You're not going to make your court of assholes pick on me either. No more of this concubine nonsense. Understood?"

Now Zale is laughing so hard he bends in two, holding his stomach. I didn't think him capable of such mirth until now. "By all the gods, Hel. You have me under your power. *Me*. And all you require is a little protection?" He tries to hold it in, bringing his hands to his mouth, but laughter roars out of him all the same. "And I called you a vixen."

"Shut up." I glance around, but the streets seem

deserted. So far. "Your theatrics are going to get us caught."

With great visible effort, he manages to hold it in, though he's still looking at me like I'm the best court jester he's ever had.

It would be so easy. Ten inches at most. Just one move and I'd be rid of him forever.

Grinding my teeth, I bring the point of my blade closer to his skin, daring to graze it.

My dagger is sharp. A trickle of blue runs along the silver. Now I'm the one smiling.

"If I'm to help you, I'll be left alone once you're back on your stupid throne." No, left alone isn't good enough. "Safe. *Protected*."

"Fine," he says easily. "No gold, no title, no position for you, for saving your king's neck. Only protection. If you insist on being short-sighted, who am I to deter you?"

"Swear it," I demand.

I won't let him use me and do as he pleases on the other side. If I'm really going to risk my skin taking care of his spoiled ass until things calm down, then by all hells, I'll have his word.

I don't like his smirk. I definitely don't trust the way he's looking at me now. Like he's the one with the upper hand, when I hold a dagger, when I'm the one who can navigate the underbelly of the city he doesn't truly know.

"You'll have to do the same," he says. "If you want my word, I want yours. You'll do your best to get me out of the city and back to safety, yes?"

I narrow my eyes, trying to see his angle. He has one, I can sense it. In the end, I nod, because that's fair. A simple bargain. My help now—his, later.

He lifts his hand to mine, entirely ignoring the blade I carry. "So long as you're true to your word, I, Zale Devar, king of Ravelyn, will protect you, Helyn Stovrj-Rhodes, against harm. Your enemies will face my wrath. By my troth, I swear it."

That sounds a little too formal, and it's also more than what I asked, but I'll take it.

"Your turn. My word won't be binding until you return the vow, little fox."

I hate him.

"I, Hel Stovrj, promise to..." I don't know what to say. I have to be careful of the wording, as he ensured his word would only be valid if I keep mine, to the letter. "Do my best to keep you alive, and bring you to safety." There, that should work. No more or less than what I intended. "By my troth, I swear it."

He seems satisfied.

A little too satisfied.

Or he's only trying to mess with me. It wouldn't be the first time. I should have requested he stop doing that, too.

His free hand moves a little too fast, turning my wrist and grasping the hilt of the dagger.

"Come on, vixen. You know what a formal vow with a demi entails. Unless you're scared of a little blood."

I roll my eyes.

He was first to speak, so I have to be first to bleed. I let him take the dagger.

I expect him to cut deeper than necessary, somewhere that'll hurt. It's the last time he can hurt me. I'm surprised Zale chooses the back of my wrist, and barely even presses the blade as he slices. My blood lines the shallow wound, embarrassingly red.

I'm proud of being common. To him, to his kind, it's but a weakness.

I return the courtesy, slicing him in the same spot—left wrist, a shallow wound that wells blue.

I press my wound to his, wincing as the now-familiar coat of magic envelops us, warm and foreign.

By the time we're done, his wound closes up again, whereas mine will take days to heal. It doesn't matter. We've still exchanged blood. Our promises are binding in a primal sense. If either of us knowingly chooses to break them, we'll die.

Although Zale might well be cruel enough to choose to die just to piss me off.

I wince. "What the hell?" The wound is burning me, white hot though it was so small.

I turn my wrist and gasp. Before my eyes, I see my skin closing up. The simple straight line of blood moves to form a complex and strangely beautiful design around my wrist.

The pain fades, and I'm healed in seconds, but the design remains, branded on my skin in sky-blue ink.

I glare at Zale. "You branded me?"

He shrugs. "Well, that's a permanent vow. I could

have left it as a boring old scar, but what's the fun in that?"

I want to punch him, but I consider that could go against the promise I just made. I don't want to die just to get even.

"You're an ass." I roll my eyes, pretending he isn't getting to me. "Let's go."

He doesn't protest as I jump back to shore, and take off down the streets, toward the only place that makes sense.

My part of the city.

CHAPTER THIRTY-EIGHT

WITHIN FOUR WALLS

I 've only seen Helyn move like this twice, once on that first night in the garden, and in my maze. Up here in the city, she's faster, never hesitating as she scales ten-foot walls or leaps to a roof yards away. I can barely keep up, though I'm better trained and part fae. I don't doubt she's stealthier.

She rebuffs my every attempt to speak with a stern look, and makes me crouch low, wait, and hide several times.

I push all thought of the attack away and focus on the moment. Explosions can still be heard all over the city. The priority is my safety and Helyn's. We need to return to Ravelyn and plan retaliation from a position of strength. Remaining caught as a bargaining ship for the brutes is out of the question.

At least I ensured that if I am taken, there's a future path for my realm, a successor to my throne.

She won't have it easy. Half of the coldbloods will try to manipulate her, and the other half's likely to stab her in a dark alley. I know enough about Helyn to trust she'll manage. Despite my best effort, she has enough allies and admirers to withstand the storm.

If we both live through this and reach our destination, she'll give me an earful once she understands what I tricked her into.

I grin, eyes on the fresh mark at her wrist.

I shouldn't be having as much fun as I am, given the circumstances, but I refuse to let myself think of all those in the arena. Reiks, his woman, my regents, my guards. I have to believe they found their way out. And if they didn't, now isn't the time to mourn their loss.

"We'll have to wait for dark," Hel whispers low, sitting on the flat roof of a two-story building at the corner of a sinuous avenue.

I join her as she closes her eyes. Her entire body remains on alert, tense.

"You can sleep, you know. I'll stand guard."

She snorts. "Right. Because you're so street smart."

She has me there.

I was schooled in warfare, in dueling and games of strategy. Our evasive escape is far from the behavior of a proper king, though it kept my head on my shoulders and laser-hole free, so I'm willing to adapt.

"I can sense people before you'd ever see them. There are..." I focus one moment. "About a hundred people in this street and the next one, all of their auras tinted by a degree of fear." A humorless chuckle escapes. "And excitement. Almost half of them...they like what happened uptown."

Helyn's green eyes cut through to mine. "Live in the

gutter long enough, and you'd be excited by the prospect of change, too."

My jaw tightens.

Slaughtering some of us with the element of surprise is easy enough, but in an open war, the commons would suffer, and die by our hands. They must see that. If Hel's presence hadn't held me back, I would have killed anyone standing within half a mile simply by manipulating the temperature around me, and I'm *one* demi. With enough time to prepare and spells at the ready, they don't stand a chance. "That's not how you get change."

"No, it's not," she agrees, to my relief. "But I was there at the council. Zale."

I don't think she's called me by name before, not once. I feel it to my bones.

"I was there today during the council session. How your kind speak of the rest of us...it's disgusting. Our welfare isn't even discussed. You talk of us like we're nothing but silly pets who can't understand anything. That's what started the violence. Not the commons. Your indifference."

I don't answer because for my part at least, she's right.

I have been indifferent to commons. Worse than indifferent—willfully neglectful.

A few dozen of them wronged me and if I ever thought of the suffering of their kind, it was with pleasure. I can't even say I've had a change of heart toward the mortals in general. Any difference in me was brought on by the woman by my side, and if I want to help, it's for her sake more than theirs.

"After we get out of this mess and return home, you can sit on my council and ensure those matters are discussed. You can even present them to the next session, after the Hall of Peace is rebuilt."

Hel huffs. "Like anyone will listen to me."

"I'll make them listen."

I don't think she believes me, but I mean every word.

Valina was right. I'm not the kind of person who can think for an entire realm, especially one as vast and diverse as mine. I lack the empathy. What I can do is follow the lead of someone who actually has a beating heart.

We watch the sunset in the distance, hidden behind a thick cloud of smoke. The city stinks of ashes. There's no longer any ruckus to be heard, which means the rebels have had their fill of slaughter for now, and in the silence, my kind is preparing to retaliate.

"Come on."

Hel climbs down the side of the building and crosses the street to a smaller house with a blue door she pushes through with her shoulder.

The weak wood gives in at the first shove. She winces and rubs her arm.

"Next time, let me be the muscles, m'kay?" I walk into the small space. "At least for my ego."

She snorts, locking the door again. "There's a trick to that door, you have to shove and push upward at the same time."

How does she know that?

I look around, and I know immediately.

The room's tidy and an utter mess all at once—the surfaces are bare, but the shelves are full of potions ingredients and books, so...

"This is your house."

The open space serves as a kitchen, library, and dining room, cluttered and charming. The plywood shelves are painted a cheerful blue with flowers and mushrooms drawn along the side.

The entire thing could fit seven times in my entry hall.

"Grandma Lyn's." She thinks a moment. "Well, I suppose it is my house. She died earlier this summer."

I can feel, just from this room, and the mixture of sadness and nostalgia in her weak smile, that she was loved here.

"I should give it away."

"Why?"

"I don't need it, and some family could use a roof over their head for winter." It's as simple as that for Hel. She'd give up this place where she grew up simply because it will help someone. I can't even begin to comprehend such selflessness.

She gets busy, full of nervous energy, shuffling pots and pans until she gets some water on the ancient gas stove.

There's very little technology to be seen in this house, not even an electric kettle. I see light switches along the wall panels, but Hel chooses to light a candle instead.

"Anything I can do to help?"

She shoots me an evaluating glance, as if wondering what I'd be good for. It's a valid question. I have seldom warmed my own water, but the rare times I did, it wasn't on an antique set-up. If she gives me a task, I'm not certain I'll be qualified to complete it.

"There should be an old e-stone upstairs, in the larger bedroom." She doesn't sound certain. "See if you can find it to send a message to your people. They could land in a hovercraft nearby to get you back to Ravelyn."

I don't miss how she pointedly excludes herself.

The narrow staircase, immured under a low ceiling, gives me an uncomfortable sense of encasement, though I've never been claustrophobic—or perhaps I've just never had to stand in so small a space before. I skip two or three steps at a time to get upstairs faster, arriving in a corridor ending in a pink door, with a yellow one to the side.

I open the latte, first, and take in everything, from the small cot, to the tidy, cramped bookshelves. There's a plushie shaped like a black-winged dragon gathering dust on a small desk.

I can't imagine Helyn in here, though it must have been her room, once. She's comfortable in one of the greater courts, going toe to toe with me, and this is where she's from.

I file away yet another piece of the unending puzzling that baffles me more and more each time I unwrap another one of her secrets.

The pink room is slightly larger, and more chaotic,

so it must have been her grandmother's. Feeling like a grave robber, I approach the small bed. It's only a little larger than the one in the other room, and might fit two.

Like everything in this dollhouse, it's covered in a thin layer of dust, and a spider has taken up residence close by.

I open the nightstand and find potions and smoking herbs, as well as a small bottle of cheap liquor.

I move to the painted chest and chuckle at the underthings in the top drawer. The grandma must have led an interesting life, to favor red lace and silky things.

I find what I need next, atop a number of wooly cardigans.

Helyn didn't misrepresent the device when she said the thing was old. E-stones are paper thin and equipped with holographic technology these days. This one must weigh at least five pounds, and has a display screen instead of projectors. I haven't seen anything like it outside of tech history books.

I jump back down the stairs. "Does this thing even work?"

"I guess you'll have to find out." Helyn has something on the stove, and I can't help but wonder at the strange domestic situation we find ourselves in; I, the king, who hasn't wandered in kitchens since I used to stalk the cook for cheese puffs, and she, the library rat. "You had some food here?"

"Don't get excited. Grandma Lyn didn't have much in her pantry, but I had to chuck most of it away. This, Your Highness, is a can of lentil soup."

"Soup. Canned." I know the meaning of both words but they don't make sense put together.

"If it offends your sensibilities, you don't have to eat."

My neglected stomach grumbles in protest. "Smells good."

I join her by the kitchen, lowering the device to the island separating the area from the dining room. To my wonder, it switches on when I press a discrete button on its side. A bright screen greets me, along with a hundred pings denoting updates. "You know your grandmother's password?"

She wrinkles her nose. "No clue. I don't use these things if I can help it."

My brow furrows. "Why?"

It's not unusual for demis to avoid e-stones and other technology. Technology is almost exclusively designed by common folks, in order to gap the bridge between our kind and theirs.

I can't deny some of it is useful—transports, lighting, the global network—but our kind would have been content to remain in candlelight. Our vision is stronger, our hearing, more acute. Most demis are long-lived and only think to bear children in their third or fourth century. In the days of my father, there were little to no electric devices available. We reap the benefits when it suits us, but we don't tend to work to further tech.

E-stones, some of their latest inventions, are particularly ill-suited to our kind. I'm not sure whether by design or because of the nature of the eldritch arts, but scanning, photographing, or even recording some spells is enough to make devices explode. I've fried more than one e-stone just by casting a spell close to it.

It makes no sense that Hel would have such issues.

She shrugs. "I don't know. They always give me a headache. I think it's the lighting."

That's the final real clue I get about the nature of Helyn Stovrj.

My jaw opens and closes. I would never have thought of it, because most people like her are defective, freaks of nature.

"I know what you are."

Finally.

CHAPTER THIRTY-NINE
THE KING'S CHOICE

"I'm a common," I reply automatically, pouring the soup into two wooden bowls.

Zale is annoyingly fixated by the notion that I have to be something else in order for him to consider me his equal. That misconception stems from his dislike of my kind, and I refuse to indulge his fantasy.

I slide one of the bowls to his side of the kitchen isle with a spoon.

He surprises me by thanking me first, and then agreeing with me. "Well, yes, in a manner of speaking."

I didn't expect him to agree so readily, but the second part of his statement is cryptic enough. I give in. "What do you mean?"

"Have you ever heard of enhancement?" His eyes widen. "Hm. That is quite good. A little too warm for comfort, but good. Canned, you said?"

I roll my eyes. "You really are a spoiled brat."

"Watch your tongue, my lady. You're talking to a

king." His words fit the arrogant ass I first met, but the tone entirely lacks the excess of pride I would have expected. "So, enhancements?"

I dip my head. "Of course. That's when witches grant abilities that aren't innate to someone, right? They usually cost a pretty penny, but Grandma Lyn helped patch up a wounded witch once. In exchange, she got a small enhancement for cheap. Just enough to brew a little magik into her remedies." Before he can ask, I add, "That was just a few years ago, decades after she gave birth to my mother. I didn't inherit her gifts. Nor have I purchased any."

"It's a misconception to think enhancements are the trade of witches. The term was first coined about a century ago, when common-born parents first gave birth to children with abilities. Some could run as fast as cats, others had the strength of a bear. Some had scales for skin or gills on their abdomens." Zale blows over his bowl, and I watch thick steam rise and dance in the air. "All let their skills get to their head, misused them against their peers or challenged the wrong demi. They rarely lived long."

My nostrils flare. "And you think I'm like those people, is that it?"

"I think you're better, vixen." Cooler now, he devours his meal in a few spoonsful. "Enhancements were nature's answer to the presence of demis in the lives of the common—an attempt to balance the scale. Failed attempts," he allows. "Until you. I should have guessed as much long ago, but your aversion to technology is what tipped me off." He taps the flat surface of my grandmother's stone. "I read about someone like you once. She went mad and scratched her eyes out."

"That's reassuring," I chuckle.

"As I said, you're an improvement. The girl used to take in whatever information she saw, all of it, all at once—everything anyone said at any given time, every word she read. And she processed it, analyzing it all like a machine."

I hadn't taken him seriously at first, but that catches my attention. "What happened to her?"

"Tech." He tilts his chin to the e-stone. "It was invented in her time, and she couldn't even look at it. Her brain was analyzing every line of code, each bit of information that made the device function."

I don't know what to say. I've always thought of myself as one thing and he's telling me I'm something else entirely, describing the way my brain works in greater detail than I ever have. I could pretend not to believe him, but what's the point? As he said, I process information, and this adds up.

I decide I don't have to process it today. I have enough on my plate. "Try my birthday for the password?" I recite the date and he punches it in, unlocking the device on the first try.

I direct my attention away from the screen and finish my soup.

His expression soon sours.

"What's going on?"

"I can't get through to my guards. I knew communication wasn't going through." Zale touches a spot behind his ear. "I couldn't contact them earlier. But I should see someone—anyone—online. I'm reluctant to leave my location in a message without knowing what's going on."

"Better not," I agree. "The bedrooms are upstairs. It's small, and maybe a little dirty, but no one will think to look for you here. We can catch some rest, sleep on any decision. Your guard might be available by morning."

As soon as I'm done with my soup, I gather the bowls and take them to the sink.

Zale takes a nearby cloth and sets to drying as I wash. He's terrible at it, but I appreciate his attempt.

"What would your court think if they saw you like this?" I tease. "Why, they may take you for a servant."

"But I am. A servant of the kingdom of Ravelyn."

I can only snort.

Pots, pans, and utensils tidied, I stand awkwardly, having nothing left to do to occupy my hands or my mind. On impulse, I open the treat cupboard. The cookie jar rattles when I set it aside, so I check it and empty its contents in the trash. I wash my hands and with a grin, retrieve a smaller jar, filled with Grandma Lyn's candied violets.

She made them herself in their winter blooms and they can last several years.

The first taste of tangy sweetness is a trip down memory lane. "Want one?" I offer, with some reticence.

There must be a dozen blooms in the jar, and once they're gone, no one can make them again. I'm not much of a cook, but I should have asked my grandmother how to make my favorite things.

"I'm not fond of sweets."

His loss. "More for me," I delight, crunching a second in my teeth and sucking it over my tongue.

Just one more. I'll save the rest for later. I bring the next to my lip, and right before I can eat it, Zale takes my wrist in his iron grip.

My eyes widen as he brings his mouth to my fingers and takes the candy.

"I thought you didn't like sweets." Why do I sound breathless?

"I used to be one thing, hold certain habits, and never questioned them." He lets go of my hand. "I have no idea what I like."

His admission is multilayered; he's not talking about the sweets at all.

I don't pretend I don't understand him. "So just like that, in two days, you've decided you've changed?"

Zale's already close, and he takes another step toward me. "Not so much decided as accepted."

I welcome my indignation, clinging to it with all my might.

"So, what, I'm supposed to forgive you because you decided to stop behaving like a bastard for a hot second?"

"Forgiveness isn't what I'm after."

I don't get to ask him what he's after, because his mouth has crashed against mine and I can't form a coherent thought, let alone words.

CHAPTER FORTY

CIRCLES OF MADNESS

Two days ago, his kiss was almost unwilling, tentative at first. Now Zale takes my mouth like he has a right to it. Like it belongs to him. I let him.

I have the sense, and the strength, to stagger back. "No. You don't get to touch me because you've decided I'm worthy."

When he thought me nothing but a common, I disgusted him. Now, he has a theory to cling to explaining away my normalcy, and all of a sudden he's interested?

I take a step back at his approach, not trusting myself, and my back hits the stove.

"I don't want you because you're enhanced." He stops advancing, but brings his cold hand to my face, twining one of my curls around a finger. "I want you because you look like sin and taste like sunshine. I want you because you've ridden my dreams and nightmares since I first saw you. I'm sorry I fought you. I'm sorry I fought myself. You were always the same magnificent, perceptive, ridiculously bookish creature. The only difference is me."

His words are exactly what I've always wanted from him, this validation, the acknowledgement of my worth his scorn has denied me. For all that, I should still tell him it's far too little, much too late. He's wounded me again and again, going for the throat and when that failed, stabbing at my heart in his search for a weakness.

He is my enemy because he wished it so. Can my pride allow for him to decide that our fight is over now?

I'm already struggling to think, but his hand glides along my shoulders, then travel the length of my arm.

"You suck." My retort is weak, but it's all I have.

"I'll spend a hundred years making up for it," he promises.

I'm about to tell him I'll be dead in a hundred years, but he's taken my mouth again.

His commanding kiss and the light touch of his hands could drive me insane with yearning. I run my fingers through his soft hair, treating him like he's mine to play with. Mine to savor. Mine to tease. I nip at his lower lips and he snaps. Zale takes both of my thighs below the knees and lifts me up on the wooden countertop. I wrap my legs around his torso and he grunts, leaving my mouth to watch me.

Zale fists several of my curls and lowers his nose to my hair, inhaling my scent. "You want me," he says half smug, half wonder.

I wrinkle my nose. "Doesn't everyone want you?"

"No one else matters."

He can say the sweetest lies. I reward him for it with a kiss along his neck, then under his ear. Releasing his head, my hands toy with the top buttons of his black shirt, closed for once. I can count on this contrary man to have too many buttons fastened when I want them gone.

"I should have taken you in the royal chamber." Abandoning my hair, his hand skims the length of my neck, dipping lower and lower, returning to my parted thighs. "On a bed of silk and feathers, covered by roses. I should have ripped all your pearls off and claimed you then. I certainly wanted to."

"That fucking dress," I groan.

"I'll have you wear it again." Zale's finger grazes the band of my pants and slides below. "So that I can tear it from you."

I'm chuckling one moment and gasping the next.

The Ravelynian king is a shade of sinful and filth, well-schooled in the arts of pleasure. His fingers tease the nub at the apex of my thighs, slip between my heated folds and back to my sensitive clit, featherlight, teasing as he takes my mouth, deeper, harder.

"Zale!"

He grunts against my lips, sensing my growing need in the furnace that is my core, and curves two fingers inside me, seeking my burning insides with harsh, purposeful force. My entire body tightens. My spine arches, throwing my head back and my chest forward. I pant, this foreign body of mine racing toward an inexorable release at a blinding, almost painful speed.

Zale's free hand slips underneath the fabric of my tunic to seek one of the taut, sensitive breasts that I didn't realize were crying for attention. I scream when he touches them, ever so soft and gentle. Then he drags the entire top up, bunching the fabric over my bare breasts, and lowers his mouth to one of my hard, pointed nipples. I don't understand how his cold skin can burn me, but it does.

I'm not in control of any of my limbs, flailing helplessly like I'm a puppet under someone else's strings.

In and out, faster and faster, his fingers take me, and his thumb runs in slow, lazy circles at my clit. And his mouth. And his hand cupping my breast. It's all too much, and I can't control it. I tumble over the precipice, with a scream.

Zale moves my limp, slack body against his chest, and carries me upstairs. I don't even attempt to move until he's lowered me to my familiar bed.

Then I blink in surprise.

"Sleep," he tells me, kissing the top of my head.

Though weary, sleep holds no appeal for me as I watch him stand to leave.

I've never been this thoroughly fucked, and Zale is still entirely dressed and too composed. I didn't even manage to undo more than three of his buttons.

That won't do at all.

Before he can turn to leave, I hook my finger in the top of his pants and sit up. He's so ridiculously tall, but with the added height of my bed, I reach his crotch on my knees.

"Helyn." There's a warning in his tone, and the way his blue eyes change to green.

I choose not to heed it, making quick work of his one silver button and his zipper next. His hard cock springs free, pointing straight where I want it.

He's larger than life everywhere, but still, his cock is the most ridiculous part of him, too long and thick, curving upward proudly. Perfect.

Pale fingers brush under my chin and lift my head so that I look straight into his bright green eyes, ripe with magik. "You don't need to do this."

I keep my gaze fixed on his and open my mouth, wrapping my lips around his thumb first. "I very much do, Zale. I may expire if I don't have you in my mouth right now."

His jaw ticks with what I would have interpreted as anger days ago.

Zale lets go of my face, and I open my mouth wide to take him in. His tip is large enough to fill my mouth —I curl my tongue around his folds, and am rewarded by a low growl.

I've taken half a dozen cocks in my mouth, and none posed the kind of challenge his does. There's no chance in hell I can fit him all in.

Titling my head back and gaping wider, I suck in what I can, and curve both of my fists around the rest, twisting his length in my grasp, slow and firm. Heat pools between my legs as he hisses. I blow. I lick. I pump, and lower my fingers to his base to seize his balls, too. I worship his massive cock in any way I can think of, taking my time exploring every inch of it.

Zale calls my name, reverently at first, then warningly, pleadingly. I ignore it all and return the delicious torture he submitted me to.

My insides clench uncomfortably with need, until I have to move one hand between my legs to quiet the yearning in my groin.

Zale catches the movement and grunts a protest. He steps back from my mouth, and I pout. "I wasn't done."

"Trust me. Nor was I."

Pushing against my chest until I lean back against my old bed, he unfolds the legs tucked under my ass and peels my trousers down my thighs, then helps me out of my tunic. I sit back, almost naked but for flimsy silk panties, and he watches, still dressed, his crotch and half of his shirt open. There's something lewd to his still wearing clothes, with his hard, glistening cock right there, but when he decides to even the scales, I certainly don't complain.

He reveals his lean, scarred, sculpted torso, opening his shirt, and then lowers his slacks along his strong legs. My folds throb with need. "Don't tease."

I shouldn't have said that. Now, all he does he tease.

He kneels on my bed and his strong hands part my knees, but he just runs his finger at the corner of my panties, barely ever grazing the heat where I need him most. His mouth kisses the length of my thigh, my stomach, and my breast.

"Please, Zale."

"You're not making yourself come. No one else is. From now on, only me."

I narrow my eyes. "In your dreams."

He's not about to dictate what I do with my own body. Touching myself in the shower is one of the only ways I relax.

"Only me," he repeats. "Every time you want to be touched, you'll come to me, any hour day or night, and I will satisfy you. I'll touch and lick and fuck you as much as you can bear. Then, more."

His tongue sets the fabric aside and travels the length of my soaked entrance.

Oh.

"Tell me," he says against my flesh. "Tell me you'll let me worship you."

If he thinks for one second—

His tongue flicks my clit, back and forth, fast and light.

"Aaah!"

Then he stops, grinning at me between my legs. "Tell me, Helyn. If you want me to make you come, that is."

"You're a monster," I whine.

He only chuckles.

"You agree to my terms? This pussy is mine, yes?"

He's infuriating, but I bob my head up and down. There isn't much I wouldn't have agreed to for more.

He finally stops torturing me, moving his skilled mouth back on me. His fingers join it, resuming their maddening ministrations. I'm panting and begging for more, rushing to the inevitable precipice again.

Zale shifts to his feet and crawls on top of me, pressing the head of his cock against my entrance. "Are you ready to come around my cock, vixen?"

"You talk too much." I wrap my arms around his neck and bring his mouth to mine again, lifting my hips in a wordless invitation.

One that he takes.

His large cock shouldn't fit, but I'm so drenched my folds swallow it eagerly. Zale enters me slowly, carefully as we share a tender kiss. Then he withdraws and slams right back into me, hard, fast, his length hitting deeper inside me. He does it again, and again, and my old bed creaks plaintively under the relentless assault. I lift my legs to his hips, and he takes them, pushing them apart and up, practically folding me in two. I would have thought it impossible, yet he's filling me up completely, hips flush against my cheeks at each thrust. I'm taking his huge length to the base, and loving every moment.

"Can you feel that, vixen? Can you feel how well we fit?" He punctuates each word with a powerful entrance, ramming into me.

"I feel it. I feel it!" He's ruining me for any other man. Now that I've had him, the awkward, fumbling encounters I'm used to aren't even worth the bother.

My legs start to shake and my inside burns hotter, raw need practically blinding me. I'm so, so very close, but Zale draws himself out. Before I can protest, he shifts me under him, and drags my hips up to him, taking me from behind.

This isn't fucking as much as a primal, animalistic

coupling, the mindless rutting of beasts. As he barrels into me, his hand reaches out between my legs, to rub my sore, aching folds.

I lose it, coming again, falling forward with the violence of my all-consuming orgasm. Zale fucks me through it, dragging out the blinding waves of pleasures for longer. He grinds into me mercilessly while I moan weakly, and finally, with one last yell, grows impossibly larger inside me, and coats my inside with warmth.

I fall asleep before he unsheathes himself.

CHAPTER FORTY-ONE
FRIENDS AND FOES

I wake remembering exactly the reason why my inside aches, and I brace myself for awkwardness, or perhaps some indifferent cruelty.

Instead, cocooning my back, Zale brushes his lips over my shoulder. "I didn't want to wake you. I've had word."

I don't know when he went down to grab Grandma Lyn's e-stone, but it's resting on my windowsill, close to the tiny bed we share.

I blink away sleepiness, the objectively more important events of yesterday coming to mind.

The attack. The screams. The deaths, no doubt.

"Good word?"

I need a toothbrush and a shower, not necessarily in that order, but Zale doesn't seem to mind. He hovers on top of me and presses his mouth to mine, coxing my lips open.

"I'm yucky. It's morning."

"Good thing I'm yucky too, Hel." He kisses away all my protests, and my skin shivers with awareness again.

"Aren't we supposed to get you back to some throne?"

"Later."

I can't argue with that impeccable logic, with his hands doing what they do best.

He opted to forgo awkwardness altogether and fuck me slowly, thoroughly, another time.

In the shower—thankfully warm, I wasn't sure the house would still have a functional boiler—he finally let me know the city's quiet again. Some demis pushed back against the rebels, who retreated when faced with magiks, as I knew they would. Koll, my guard, was wounded trying to get to me in the square, and some of Zale's men were crushed under the collapse of the Hall of Peace.

No one is likely to forgive, or forget last night anytime soon.

As I dress in one of Grandma Lyn's hand-sewn sundresses, the only clean option I have in this house, I wonder where this thing between Zale and I will go, when he'll rage against my kind and I'll tell him what he needs to hear: that the demis are responsible for the hatred, the violence. That things need to change on Xhera if both castes are to coexist without attempting to murder each other.

Nowhere, in all likelihood, but I'll enjoy it while it lasts. Grandma Lyn taught me that men come and go, each one right for a time. When we part ways, I'll be fine.

I will.

I charter a ride on the globe, using the main city craft provider, rather than giving my location to my guard. This house is Hel's, and I will not have its placement known to more people than necessary. For one, who knows when we might need a hideout again?

"The hovercraft will be here in five," I say.

I can think of a million different ways to make use of those few minutes, but Helyn's writing short letters. Instead of disrupting her, I watch her, face scrunched up in concentration, biting her lip.

"Anything I can help with?" I ask when I can bear to interrupt her.

She shakes her head, eyes staying on her work. "I'm almost finished. Just letting Alva know she can let anyone who needs it use the house, and telling the utilities to bill me, so they keep the water and heat, that sort of thing."

I can't pinpoint why I don't like any of this at first. "You grew up here. Don't you want to keep it, visit it when you feel like it?"

I might have used the Whyte Fort for years, but the Dark Keep is my home.

"Maybe," she admits. "But I haven't come here in

the last ten weeks. I'd rather it house a family in need than sit empty for the sake of nostalgia."

While I understand her, I don't want her to sacrifice anything. "Keep the house. I'll build a shelter ten times its size, if it makes you feel better."

She frowns up at me. "A new shelter would be nice. But when it's full, someone might need the house too. You underestimate the poverty of the undercity if you think one act of goodwill can fix it."

I don't underestimate anything—I'm fully aware that I know nothing of her neighborhood, save for its reputation for crime and debauchery. "It's my offer: you keep the house, I build a shelter. Take it or leave it." I'll have her keep a piece of joy for herself, even if I have to barter for it.

Hel's jaw tightens. "Fine," she grumbles, crumpling one piece of paper in her hand. "Happy?"

"Exceedingly." I glance at the time. "Let's be on our way."

"To Ravelyn?" She hesitates. "I should stay in the city. Check on the Rhodeses." Her nose wrinkles as she says it, her loyalty reluctant but there nonetheless.

"I called a meeting, and as my regent, your stepfather will be there." That is, if he's alive. I didn't think to enquire about his welfare when I contacted the palace. "The fighting may be over, but I'll feel better if you're out of the city for the time being, Hel."

She sighs and nods, though grudgingly. I can't be surprised at her lack of enthusiasm, given that I threw her in my labyrinth and dressed her in my mother's pearls on her last visit. "It won't be like your last time in the Whyte Fort. I won't torture you." I stop to think one moment. "Much."

"You don't have to. Your weather will do it for you."

I remember how she suffered in the Devar house, mild as the temperature is. My country must have been unbearably cold to her over the weekend.

"You have my protection, remember? You'll be fine."

She's doubtful, but she joins me all the same. We leave the house by the front door, in daylight this time. I get to see the gray-paved sinuous street, the sandy small houses stacked like hay, with colorful doors and tiny square windows. The street might have been picturesque in a romantic painting, but from here, I smell the stench and feel the blinding heat, so much heavier than in the rest of the city, with so many people enclosed in small quarters.

The ride I order stands out, sleek and matte black. The driver's parked a little farther down the street, as it gets too narrow this far up. A small crowd has gathered around it, admiring the model. One man stands out to me, dressed under a cloak, holding himself straight a few steps away from the hovercraft, eyes looking straight at us.

"Khel!" Hel calls, smiling. "I'm glad to see you here. How's Alva, and the rest?"

She starts to walk toward him, and I tense.

If there's one thing I'm good at by right of nature, it's reading people, and this man holds a shadow. I trail her steps close, my attention glued to the man.

"Well. She took no part in the fight yesterday."

I note that he says nothing of himself.

The man, quite handsome and a little older, looks up to me pointedly.

Hel clears her throat. "This is Zale. Zale, Khel. We're on our way out, but I'll check on the Claws very soon."

Claws? I have so many questions, none of which I want to ask here and now.

The man doesn't say anything, staying planted between us and the transport. I take Hel's hand and start to lead her away. "We're late."

Helyn shoots me a forbidding glance, not understanding my unease in front of her friend.

At least not until his hand darts out under his cloak and brings a dagger to her throat.

CHAPTER FORTY-TWO

THE BLOOD OF KINGS

I don't understand why Khel, my oldest friend, the one who showed me how to unlock any door, pulled a knife on me. The information doesn't compute; it defies everything I know. The Claws, and the lanes, and the commons of the undercity are supposed to be on my side, and the rest of the world against us.

Except I'm no longer a simple common, am I? I have become, if not the enemy, someone they can use.

I wonder if Alva's in on this.

"If I feel the air crackle for even a second, if you say so much as a word, I'll slit her throat before you can lift a finger," Khel sneers. "In the car, and be quick about it, Your Highness."

How does Khel know so much about Zale's power? I didn't, weeks ago.

Zale holds both hands in the air in surrender and starts to step back, slow, until he reaches the back of the hovercraft. He opens the door and slides inside.

"What are you doing?" I hiss.

I know one thing: Khel's running a job and this time, I'm the target.

"Shush. You know how this works. He'll do what we tell him, and you won't be harmed."

Khel leads me to the passenger door and tilts his chin forward. "Get in, Hel."

This can't be good. "No."

"Hel..." His tone holds an impatient warning.

I straighten my spine and stare him dead in the eyes. "I'm not letting you use me as a hostage."

I don't recognize Khel's gray gaze. It's too cold, lacking any hint of emotion. To an extent, he's always been that way, but I meet a beast different from the one I'm used to. Maybe because I'm no longer its master.

"Get in."

He doesn't bother voicing a threat, and this time, I obey.

The streets uptown are still unfamiliar to me, but as the hovercraft glides through the empty, still-dusty streets, I get a familiar vibe. At the next corner, I realize we're heading to Green Lane, my stepfather's place on Stateside. My confusion gives way to stone-cold anger when the vehicle slides past the open gate of the duke's red brick house.

I knew it. I knew that some form of betrayal would come from the Rhodeses, from my mother.

I don't know what happened yet, but if I'm sitting next to one of my oldest friends with a blade aimed at my neck, it's her doing.

"Get out, Your Majesty," Khel orders.

Zale catches and holds my gaze before obeying.

If he were alone, Khel would be dead on the floor within seconds, but with me here, he's not about to risk it. Which is why Khel made me tag along in the first place.

I need to get to his blade and move out of the way, somehow.

The blade tightens at my skin, as though he heard my thought. "Your turn. Slow and steady. I know all your tricks, Stovrj."

"I thought I knew all yours, but that was before you added betrayal to your arsenal. What are you doing?" I demand.

"You're one to talk. He made you his whore, and you protect him, Hel? Really?" Khel snorts. "As I said, I won't hurt you. It's Devar they want. And once they're done with him, we'll have everything we wanted, everything we need for the lane. A hospital, money, a school."

Oh, the idiot. "Neleda *lies*, Khel. That's all she does, as easy as breathing."

He sighs. "You don't know what you're talking about. We'll talk when it's over."

What is over? I want to ask, but he's done indulging me.

"*Out*."

I want to push, but the coldness of his eyes warns

me not to. I get out of the hovercraft, and follow after Zale.

Khel shifts the blade to my back, between my shoulder blades, and we walk in silence to the house.

Each time I entered it, I was greeted by footmen and bright lights. The butler was never far, nor were the servants, ready to provide refreshments. Now, it is still and silent.

"To the right," Khel tells Zale, directing him to the duke's bar.

Zale stops at the entrance and looks over to me with concern before crossing the threshold.

I enter and gasp.

My mother and the duke are both present, though both are tied to chairs, hands bound behind their backs. Neleda's eyes widen when she sees me, and she fights against the ropes in vain.

Her mouth is gagged, but the duke's isn't. She must have run her mouth, as we Stovrj are wont to do.

"What's the meaning of this?" Zale demands.

I was so focused on the odd, unexpected sight of my mother in chains, I didn't notice her jailers. I don't recognize the three men at first, though I can tell at first glance all are coldbloods, with their pale skin and the general aura surrounding them.

Then I do identify one of them, the oldest-looking one, still thin and glowering; he's the duke's butler who hated me so.

"This," the man snarls, "is comeuppance."

Khel drops the dagger at my back, and takes my

shoulders, leading me to one of the empty chairs. "Stay here if you know what's good for you."

He doesn't bother to bind me, but he remains close, with the hilt in his hand.

"I don't know who you are, and I do not care." Zale's voice is slow and low. I can hear the contained rage. "You will release Helyn and her family this instant, or face suffering a thousandfold before I grant you the mercy of death."

The butler chuckles. "Hear him roar, the little king. He's a true Devar, all right." He shows his teeth. "You shouldn't have made it. You should never have survived then."

"Givon, this is madness," the duke roars. "Zale isn't responsible for what happened to you, for what happened to any of us."

"He's a selfish tyrant, like his father. And look at who he's brought to his bed: a lowborn, common swine. Just like you." The butler practically shakes with fury. "You don't deserve to rule."

"Whoever told you ruling was about deserving anything?"

The butler crosses the room till he stands in front of Zale and strikes him, hard and fast, the punch resounding through the room.

Zale chuckles and spits ice-blue blood. "Givon," he says. "I know that name. I remember that song."

The butler lifts his hand again and this time, Zale's ready: he catches his wrist and moves to twist it behind his back. The butler moves with both speed and agility, freeing his hand.

Zale's hand lifts at the level of butler's face, and crushing to fist the air, calling to his magik. The other man's hand mirrors the gesture. Two pointed spears made of ice appear out of thin air, hurtling at great speed, one toward Zale, the other, the butler.

And both men block them with a wave of their hands.

Zale's cruelest smile crosses his face. "Hello, brother."

CHAPTER FORTY-THREE
OLDEN SONGS

T dismissed the story as an old wives' tale designed to keep scared children in line when I first heard it, but that name. Those eyes. That power. I'd know it anywhere.

My father lived six hundred years, and in all his time, he fathered many children. The tale sang that before my elder brother Vyron, there was a boy called Givon who dared defy the king's wishes, so the king, his own father, cursed him to age, cursed him to die, and never rule the land that belonged to him by right.

And here he is, my brother, a man older than I ever will be, forty seasons from the grave at most.

It is strange to see what I'd look like if I were to age. I'm glad such decay isn't in the cards for me.

"Givon, this is madness," the duke pleads. "The crown cannot go to you, even if you kill the king. Your father ensured that."

The crown of Ravelyn is a sentient thing, enchanted by my ancestors to avoid situations like this:

only the natural successor of the previous king can take it.

If my father truly had Givon struck from the line of succession, no amount of bloodshed can earn him the reins of the kingdom. At my death, the next in line would be the Rhodeses, the Adlers, and the Greystones, not him.

"I don't care if I never rule," my brother fumes. "So long as this boy doesn't destroy our kingdom like his father attempted to. You saw what he did! He named *her* his concubine. He had proud, great lines, but insults it and gave her the secrets of our founder's maze!"

These are excuses, and weak ones at that. I pay them little mind.

My eyes fall on Harl Greystone next. "And I suppose you wish to claim the crown after he kills me."

My regent snarls. "You're just like your father. You defiled my wife for your entertainment. After yesterday, no one knows where you are. They'll think the rebels killed you."

"A good plan," I admit.

It only has one flaw. They're relying on their hostages to stay my hand, believing I won't strike and risk harming Helyn.

Before yesterday, they might have been right.

I have only one weakness in the room, and while her name is Stovrj, it isn't Helyn.

I'll kill her mother if I have to, though.

"You had my family killed." It's not a question.

"*Our* family, I suppose," I amend. I look at Harl, and then Otto Nettlestein. "And you helped him."

"The king was a beast," Otto mutters, glancing at his feet. "We didn't order the children or the ladies to suffer, Your Highness. We never would have."

No, they wouldn't.

My gaze returns to my elder brother. "That order came from you."

He was banished as a boy, stripped of his birthright, and whatever trials he lived through turned him into this acrimonious beast.

"You shouldn't have survived," my brother repeats.

But once I did, Valina's protection and the protests from his accomplices forced him to stay his hand. Until now. This rebellion was too good an opportunity to pass up. They can dispose of me and call it a common crime.

Almost perfect...

"But I did. While your men murdered your father, his wives, innocent women, and all of your siblings. When the pain got too much, I froze, in fear and torment. You know, I still heard all of it—our six-year-old younger sister's screams as they raped her. The stench has never left me." I let wrath surround me, infuse my spirit. "And when they burned our corpses and danced around the pyre, I lay still. I think it took me five days to emerge. A whole season passed before I could say a word. Do you know how I get to sleep at night, while the screams and the smells haunt my dreams?" I tilt my head. "I think of vengeance."

I'm ready.

The only thing staying my hand is Helyn's poor, trembling mother.

I glance at the redheaded beauty seated next to her treacherous friend, willing her to understand me.

Get your mother out. Free Neleda. Right now.

First I see surprise in her wide green eyes, then she inclines her head once, discreetly.

I see the man at her side catch our exchange and frowns, but I don't have time to account for it. And if I know one thing, it's that Helyn can take care of herself.

My hand flashes forward and grasps my brother's throat before unleashing the power of my crown, the power of my kingdom, and the will of the ruling god of shade, as only a king could.

That's when the screaming starts.

I watch as Zale summons a blinding light, feeling the bite of coldness, the fury of gods, and the darkness of night in one single spell. His brother screams and thrashes against the hold.

Neleda.

Zale's instructions were clear, and for once, I'm not going to question them.

I rise to my feet, only to find Khel's blade pointing at me again. "Make him stop. Tell him to stop!"

I don't think I've ever heard him sound so panicked. I never thought I'd enjoy it so much, but then again, I also didn't think he was such a cunt.

Glad to have packed my dagger, I draw it out of the only place I could fit it in this sundress: my boots. I wouldn't have risked it while Khel was composed—he's far more proficient than I with a blade—but right now, he's terrified and distracted. I strike without hesitation, hitting right over his ribs, and watch as surprise crosses his face.

He's the first man I killed, and I'm surprised to not feel much of anything. His betrayal erases any sort of guilt.

Zale's urging was rather pressing, and I don't have time to waste on traitors, so I rush to my mother, cutting the bonds at her back with my bloody dagger.

What was it the old king told me in the heart of the maze? *Take the dagger. It'll serve you better than any crown.*

As I free my mother, I know without a doubt that smug Zale lookalike knew exactly what was going to happen today. It would have been kind if he'd given more details.

"We have to get out right now," I tell her, taking her hand and dragging her to the closest door. To my distress, it leads to a bathroom, not an exit.

Behind me the light brightens impossibly, and the cold piercing power driving it explodes.

On impulse, I close the door.

Ice pierces my skin, my entire body and my heart, colder than anything I've known, colder than the air of Ravelyn.

I should have died on the spot.

Failing death, I should be suffering, on the floor, trembling and begging for mercy.

Against all logic, I'm not.

I turn to face Zale just in time to see his brother's iced-over blue-white figure crackle and shatter in shards of ice.

The others, the coldbloods, shiver and tremble, their skin not pale, but white as snow.

The tall man who'd been the closest yells in horror. "My eyes! My eyes."

And in the middle of the room, Zale stands, surrounded by mists in shades of black and green, glowing in the heart of the darkness.

The magiks he summons dissipates when he steps toward the blinded coldblood.

"Be glad I only took your eyes, Harl. Your treachery cost a hundred lives, including that of my sister. That you did not intend to harm them is the only reason why you retain your miserable life. You are hereby stripped of all rank and titles, and your land will pass on to your heir."

"Pity, my lord! I have a family."

"You wife will be provided for. You, not so much." Done with him, Zale turns to the smaller one of the two remaining men. "You don't have any lands and titles to strip, so I'll settle for your fortune. Never darken the borders of my kingdom again, either of you."

I expected far worse. I would have done far worse. Zale was both just and fair in his edict.

He directs his gaze toward my stepfather and waves his hand.

The duke exhales in relief as his limbs return to their original shade, rather than the wan, snow-white hue.

"Will you attempt to undermine me now, regent?"

Salvar Rhodes gulps. "I'm good, my king."

I bet he is.

I open the door and sigh in relief. My mother's shivering, teeth chattering, but she's in one piece.

"Come outside, into the sunshine. Is there a coat nearby?"

I rush her to safety as the king frees the duke, who comes to care for his wife.

Only then do I turn to Zale. "How am I okay?"

I felt the lethal cold, it touched me like everyone else in this room. It just didn't harm me. That doesn't make a lick of sense.

Zale makes a face, half wince, half jocularity. "About that..."

EPILOGUE

S he stays angry at me for seven days and as many nights, though my queen does let me apologize on my knees, with my tongue, my fingers, and my cock.

It's not my fault, really. The opportunity was too good to pass up. Under any other circumstances, I would have had to earn the right to call her mine, but she asked to be safe and protected. I gave her exactly that.

So long as you're true to your word, I, Zale Devar, king of Ravelyn, will protect you, Helyn Stovrj-Rhodes, against harm. Your enemies will face my wrath. By my troth, I swear it.

By all the laws of our kind, I gave her my hand and she accepted it. She'll live as long as I, undying, untouched by age, because from the moment I said those words, she became mine.

My wife's coronation is occurring on the night of

my twenty-fifth birthday. She wears a pearl dress for me, though this one is black and green over a golden shift.

Reiks's fiancée claps the loudest, fond of Hel as she is.

The most precious gift comes from the new king of Flaur, who offers Helyn a crown of everlasting flowers. The Wicked girl at his side gets to her tiptoes and whispers to the new queen, "Any time, any day. Just give me the name, and they'll be dead by dawn."

That's as close to a present as a Dorathian assassin ever gets.

Helyn reaches her friend from the undercity and hugs her tight. I got to know Alva while we worked on the structural reform proposals we're about to present, and though she's still not fond of me, I like her well enough.

Finally, the queen of Ravelyn reaches her king. She glares at me from the other side of the dais as she did so many weeks ago, before taking my hand, just as I took hers.

She leads us to our twin thrones, each uncomfortable as the other, hers white marble, while mine is black as night.

A new era is about to start, one where I'm challenged by a woman much better than I, for the good of the realm and with the blessing of my ancestors.

"Hail to the queen!" the court shouts, as I bring her fingers to my mouth.

The End

Want More? Have you read the simultaneous story, *Tall Dark and Evil?* Stay tuned for a sample!

Note that Alexi writes under three pen names and prioritized the worlds that are well reviewed. If you would like more *Seven Kingdoms* novels, leave a word!

TALL DARK AND EVIL

T tighten my towel around my breasts, wishing I'd opted for a longer one, but my gym bag had been full.

Said gym bag disappeared right after my shower, with all my changes of clothes and my shoes. While I can't technically be certain that the culprits are the three Cs, they are generally at the heart of every successful prank pulled on me.

Chira Mallone, princess of Flaur, Caelin Esthera, the daughter of a duchess from somewhere in Anderkan, and Camil Ostra, the richest girl currently attending Five, *hate* me. I don't even know why. Two of them are demis, so it can't be racism. It used to keep me awake at night, wondering why the hell they despised me so much. Now, I don't care. All I want is for them to leave me alone.

Back to the murder. Daydreaming about it is somewhat comforting. Maybe I can brew an eversleeping potion, and slip that in their drinks rather than use a hex. That isn't murder, right?

Except I don't brew magik. I could ask Callan. He's the most proficient at potions, and he'd do just about anything to annoy Mar.

Hearing a familiar, annoying chuckle, I glance over my shoulder, but the corridor I just left still seems empty. That doesn't mean that the three Cs aren't here. They could be using an invisibility spell. None of them are seasoned witches, but they have enough money to pay one to do their bidding—as they've proven the number of times they've attacked me with various spells.

"Careful!" a woman screams.

My head snaps back to face forward, and I try to stop, but I'm running far too fast. My body hits a hard, tall surface that shouldn't have been in the courtyard. It wasn't, moments ago when I was looking.

Propelled backward with the momentum, I fall on my ass, hard enough to bruise my tailbone.

"Ouch." My legs hurt. My feet hurt. My back isn't too happy with me. I hear the sound of glass breaking against the pebbled tiles before I can focus on the disaster in front of me. There are hundreds of little white and blue bits, on and around me. I wince, for my ass as much as the thing I've clearly broken in my flight. The damage is irreparable. At least without magiks.

I look up, and up, and up again, until I meet a pair of silver-gray eyes.

Natheran Reiks's.

My mouth falls open, because he and I don't exist

in the same spheres. We don't mesh. We certainly shouldn't collide.

"Are you all right, Reiks?" a pretty woman dressed in royal blue asks, approaching the giant and fussing over him.

I'm the one on the ground, but I might as well not exist. Which is fair, given that the incident is entirely my fault.

I sit up painfully, bracing to get to my feet on bruised legs covered in shallow cuts.

Reiks shrugs off the woman's help and strolls to me, to offer a steadying hand. "Careful, there. We wouldn't want to add blood to this mess." His voice is so very deep, from up close. I don't think I heard it accurately in the chapel at the start of school.

I take his hand. It would be rude not to. I immediately regret it.

It feels wrong.

I don't like touching anyone if I can help it. It gives me too much of them. I sense what they're made of beneath the surface, and well, I quite simply don't care to have such insight on anyone here.

Especially him.

The contact is strange. Strange because I don't gain any unwanted knowledge at the touch. Strange because he feels too cold. Strange because a current of energy burns my skin, jolting me more than my fall did. I want to push him away and take three steps back. Before I do, Reiks bends to wrap one arm under my knees and secures the other around my back. He lifts me up like I weigh nothing at all. I'm as tall as some city lamp posts, not exactly a delicate flower. Though I suppose that compared to him, I could be.

With ease, he carries me to one of the benches littering the courtyard, sets me down and remains at my side, his large hands gently applying pressure on my foot, to test its flexibility.

I want to tell him to stop. I should. But he happens to be good at this. His soft manipulation soothes my aching limb.

"Reiks!" the woman shrieks, clearly offended. "We're late, and the relic's destroyed, thanks to that idiot. We have to—"

"Go." His voice is flat, without intonation, but the order doesn't leave room for argument. "I'll handle this."

"This" being me, presumably.

The woman doesn't look happy at all. She also doesn't have a choice. Given her silver and blue uniform marked with the Reiks emblem, she's one of his servants—or at least his subject. The crown prince has spoken.

Although she continues to huff, she leaves the courtyard, entering the university through the arched doorway I just burst out of.

"Do you make a habit of walking around Five naked?" he asks

Dammit. I'd completely forgotten the fact that I'm wearing a tiny towel. Thankfully, it's still secured around my flat chest.

I'm not shy. I dance naked in the woods several

times a year. But the Cs were right to guess that I would find this humiliating. I don't like standing out.

"Someone took my clothes in the rec center. I was going to get some in the common dorm," I rush to explain, then I mentally kick myself.

It's none of his business.

One of my weaknesses is that I pay attention to what people might think about me more than a Frejr should.

"I see."

I don't like being this close to Reiks. I don't honestly enjoy proximity to anyone at all. It makes me feel vulnerable. But Reiks? His presence is unnerving. It was when we were yards away. Now, it's worse.

The prince glances back at the broken pieces and sighs. "I suppose there's nothing to be done about it now."

"Sorry," I say, maybe too late. I'm not accustomed to apologizing. I don't typically do anything that necessitates it. "I heard—" He won't care what I heard. "I wasn't looking where I was going. It's my fault."

"I suppose it is." He tilts his head, watching me with rapt attention, just like he did the Strejaday of his fiancée's funeral.

"I can pay for it," I offer, not entirely confident that's the truth.

I have a generous allowance. That said, Reiks is a prince. Who knows how much his baubles might cost.

He laughs, a sound both soft and rough. I don't know him at all, but I somehow get the feeling he doesn't laugh very often. Still, I'd prefer he didn't do it at my expense.

He must have noticed my glaring, because he stops to say, "I don't think so. It was regalia of the first queen of Anderkan. The goblet spelled at her wedding, actually."

My jaw falls. *What*?

"And you were holding it in your *hands*?" I demand, practically screaming. "Why wasn't it boxed, and sealed, and spelled to be safe?"

Reiks is all casual indifference. Me? I'm panicking.

The first queen of Anderkan was a legend; a half giantess who sided with the mortal kingdoms and determined the fate of the war. Her chamber pot would be worth ten times my weight in gold. Her wedding goblet? Breaking it could easily cause a diplomatic incident between my family and Anderkan.

Throughout Xhera, there are many wedding ceremonies, but one of the traditional ones is to use one goblet spelled with the intimate vows. They drink of that same cup to seal the spell, and if one of them willingly breaks their promises, they die.

Even in ancient times, that tradition was rare because it is so binding.

The shards on the floor were priceless. *Priceless*. How could I mess up so badly?

How could *he*?

"It was protected at the palace," Reiks replies. "I was bringing it to be studied by the historical department. Not that it matters now."

But it does. A precious, unique, ancient antique is broken and it is my fault. "What can I do to help?"

He tilts his head, as though my help wasn't something he'd ever considered asking for.

"I don't want to get in trouble. I don't want *you* to get in trouble over something I did either." Part of me wonders why I'm blurting everything I'm thinking about without a moment's hesitation. That's not my style. I don't...talk. I'm the shy Frejr. The background one.

It must be sheer panic loosening my tongue.

"In trouble," Reiks repeats. Then he has the gall to smirk. "Don't you know who I am, Frejr?"

Of course I do, but princes have responsibilities, like everyone else. His had been to take care of the irreplaceable goblet. Now it's broken. When the king finds out, he's bound to take it out on Reiks.

Or on me.

"I will speak to my palace liaison and make sure she understands my carelessness broke the goblet," Reiks decides.

I open my mouth to thank him, but he's not done.

"Which means you do owe me." Letting go of my foot, he finally straightens up to his full, intimidating height. "How much...well, I'll have to get the goblet valued. But I'm not interested in your coin."

I stare at him, waiting for the axe to drop.

What could he want from me?

If he'd demanded money, I could have worked something out, somehow. Given the value of what I've destroyed, that would have meant going to my matriarch and begging her to bail me out. Valina would have done it, too. Not without making a deal with me first.

I know just what she would have asked of me. It would have cost me everything. The future I imagined for myself. The fragile control I gained over the last eleven years would have been torn out of my grasp and shattered as thoroughly as the goblet.

But there's a high chance Reiks wants the exact same thing from me.

He'll ask me to use magiks. I don't see anything else a man such as him could want me for.

"What's your name, witch?"

"Alis." I get up, tightening my towel again. I need to get out of here and find clothes. "And I don't practice, so I'm no witch." I'm quick to assure him, dreading the thought of having to change my path because of this mess.

I like my life now. It might get a little lonely, but it's mine. I control it.

Before I buried my powers, I had no control of anything.

"Alis," Reiks repeats, pronouncing my name so slowly it seems to have several extra syllables. "What are you, then?"

A fair question, but a loaded one. I can only shrug. "I'm a demi, technically, but my innate ability is unstable, so I don't use witchcraft. If I can repay you for the goblet in any other way, I will. Just no magik."

"Any other way?" he challenges, his eyes flashing with a wicked glint as they zero in on my chest.

I roll my eyes. "You don't need me to get off. You have a harem for that."

I'm not certain he does, but his father has one, so it would stand to reason.

Reiks shrugs. "I could have you join it."

I grimace in distaste. "Why would you?"

He's amused at my expense again. "Why, indeed? Well, Alis, I'm Natheran Reiks, heir of Anderkan, and from this day onward, until you've repaid the value of my ancestor's goblet, you belong to me. Agreed?"

"Err, no. That's not how it works. I need details. Estimates, both of time and value. A job description. A contract." I'm grasping at straws.

"What's the fun in that?" Reiks counters.

I want to throttle him. Nothing about today has been remotely fun to me, but he's loving this.

"No contract. As for the duration...let's say you'll serve me until the end of the year. I will not ask you to perform any witchcraft, and well, I suppose I won't demand you warm my bed either. Otherwise, you're mine. And everything you'll do for me will stay between you and I. Understood?"

I bite my lip, running all his words through my mind. "I have classes."

"As do I. I won't take you away from your work, Alis. Your free time, however..." He chuckles easily. "Let's just say you won't have much of it."

Well, it isn't like I'm doing anything groundbreaking in my spare time currently. Still, my instincts want me to protest, to find a loophole.

"Or I could go to your family for compensation."

That little snake. He has me cornered, and he knows it. "Fine!"

Then Reiks's mouth curves, slowly shattering his casual mask.

I wish I'd seen this smile before I'd agreed to anything. Before ever speaking to him. I would have run away screaming in the other direction.

Oh, it's beautiful. Devastatingly so. In that moment, he looks like a warrior of old: calculating, cruel, brutal, and merciless. The kind of man who'd do anything to get what he wants.

Reiks is terrifying.

And he's so, so not common. What I feel from him isn't just an echo, a memory of power.

I sense more.

I sense wildness.

I sense the same thing that slithers inside my chest, coiling to strike at the first sight of weakness.

He's a bound beast.

"I suppose that from now on, you're my bitch, Alis."

What the hell did I get myself into?

Tall Dark and Evil is a standalone novel happening at the same time as *A Shade of Sinful,* following Alis and Reiks.

CPSIA information can be obtained
at www.ICGtesting.com
Printed in the USA
BVHW030815150223
658553BV00016B/119

9 781839 840692